"A charming novel, full of honesty and insight, *Mailbox* is shot through with the mystery and mischief of childhood, and the struggles — and victories — of growing up. Compulsively readable."

— Meg Gardiner, Edgar Award winning author
of the Evan Delaney thrillers

"In *Mailbox*, Nancy Freund brilliantly replicates the bright flash of memory-making. In 76 vivid vignettes — some with the quick flash of a postcard, some with the depth and detail of a meditation — she gives us the life and thoughts of Sandy Drue, a precocious pre-teen working her way through a series of heartwarming and innocently profound questions. As with all of Freund's prose, there is a wonderful energy and humor to the writing. *Mailbox* is a fantastic piece of fiction and as true to life as a careful documentary."

— Michelle Bailat-Jones, Christopher Doheny
Award winning author of *Fog Island Mountains*

"In vignettes that bring to mind Sandra Cisneros' masterpiece *The House on Mango Street*, Nancy Freund's *Mailbox* tells an engaging, sensitive, and at times very funny coming-of-age story. Her protagonist, Sandy Drue, is a hyper-articulate, charming narrator, who, with a few stumbles, a couple of deaths in the family, and one crazy conflict in a haunted house, comes to understand truths about herself, her family, and the world around her. This is a book for both the young and old, parents and children. Anyone with a heart that feels and a head full of questions will find great wisdom and many warm moments to cherish in Freund's lovely tale."

— Brian Gresko, editor of *When I First Held You:
22 Critically Acclaimed Writers Talk About the Triumphs,
Challenges, and Transformative Experience of Fatherhood*

"Freund's prose is a gift. Her straightforward style comes off as simple, yet goes straight for the gut. Each chapter in *Mailbox* is a powerful story within itself, sometimes fun, sometimes serious, sometimes painful. It isn't always an easy read, but it is a very good one. I found myself falling in love with the pre-teen protagonist, Sandy Drue, and her wide-eyed vision of the world I myself grew up in — 1970s America. *Mailbox* brought me back to my own childhood, and how exactly that shaped me for the jungle of adulthood. Impatiently waiting for the next book by Nancy Freund."

— Katie Hayoz, author of *Untethered*

"An upbeat and heartwarming novel — a guide to the life of a bright pre-teen that develops with the reader into pre-adulthood, yet manages to bring out the inner child in all of us, especially those growing up in the 1970s."

— Daniela I. Norris, author of
Collecting Feathers: Tales from the Other Side

"*Mailbox* is an intriguing coming-of-age story, which manages to be poignant, sad and funny through short vignettes taken from protagonist Sandy Drue's life. Through Sandy's eyes we see not only her close family and beloved pet dog but also the wider community in the wake of the Watergate scandal. Sandy is a girl with thick skin and plenty of ideas about the world but she is still in search of The Meaning of Life, an elusive question for a 13 year old. *Mailbox* is a heartwarming novel about family, puberty, friendship, honour, life and death."

— Anna Solding, author of *The Hum of Concrete*

"Scattershot defines well this fascinating coming-of-age novel. The different stories that thirteen-year-old Sandy Drue has put into her mailbox are skillfully woven together to form a beguiling whole. From age seven, on her father's typewriter, Sandy has been writing letters to the world. Not only does she relate surprising incidents of her daily life, but also her understanding of them. This is where she wins the reader's heart. Sandy is quirky and precocious, but she is also generous and loyal. Especially mesmerizing is Sandy's relationship with her family — father, mother, and her brother Chris. One scene takes place around the dining table as it is thundering outside... The reader is right there at the table with them. There is a thunderstorm brewing both outside and inside. Sandy is taking it all in. So is the reader. The mailbox becomes a metaphor for connection, between Sandy and her family, her friends, her world. And also between Sandy and the reader. For the moment, Sandy believes that her book is over. But the reader hopes there will be another."

— Susan Tiberghien, author of
Footsteps: Falling in Love with a Frenchman

Mailbox

A Scattershot Novel of Racing, Dares and Danger, Occasional Nakedness, and Faith

Nancy Freund

Gobreau Press
Key Largo & Lausanne

Published by Gobreau Press LLC
First Printing May, 2015

Cover design and interior formatting by www.jdsmith-design.com. Author photo by Danielle Libine.

Freund, Nancy
Mailbox: A Scattershot Novel of Racing, Dares and Danger, Occasional Nakedness, and Faith/by Nancy Freund.

Paperback ISBN: 978-09887084-8-8
Ebook: 978-09887084-6-4

Gobreau Press proudly supports community and global literacy.

Please consider the following organizations: The Reader Organisation (www.thereader.org.uk), www.826valencia.org, www.litworld.org, www.roomtoread.org, and the International Baccalaureate, (www.ibo.org).

For Jane

"Only connect…" –E.M. Forster

In fact, here's what that comes from:

"Only connect the prose and the passion, and both will be exalted, and human love will be seen at its highest. Live in fragments no more." –E.M. Forster, *Howard's End*

That's not a typo for Foster.
It's Edward Morgan Forster with an "r."

Contents

1. Knothole in the Tree House

I'd never have been in the dark-dungeon tree house behind the church if the public school teachers hadn't gone on strike. Not that I'm blaming those teachers or those kids in there or the kids who left or anyone else. No one else was to blame. When you get right down to it, people make their own choices about whether to go into a terrible place or not, and that includes me.

I was in second grade. A kid can't just not go to school, so my parents changed my brother Chris and me to a private one. We had to take a test with the principal to be sure we were smart enough, and luckily we both were. I had never had an out-loud test before that. I got every vocabulary word right except "agown" which turned out not to be the word she meant. She told my mom she was surprised I didn't know "agown," even as she was telling her I was very bright. I would still say I don't know the word "agown," but of course that would be obnoxious. With every other word, she only said the word – not "a" or "the" – so how was I supposed to know she meant just *gown*, as in a lady's fancy dress? Obviously I know the word *gown*. I should have gotten 100%! But no matter how smart a person is, there can always be silly unfair things that make you miss your hundred. My mom says there are also always little things you get right when you didn't really know them, but you took an educated guess. It all balances out in the end, that's how life works. She also says, "Get over it, Sandy. Life isn't fair."

At recess when I first switched schools, some kids crammed into a kind of circle around me in the dark-dungeon tree house, all crowded and jostling, and they were asking, "What are you?"

"Nothing."

They stared at me in the dim light. I didn't know all their names yet.

"She's lying." Mark Martinez has a gruff voice, like a grown man with a sore throat, and he wears Toughskins jeans. "No one's nothing."

"Yes, they are. I'm nothing," I said.

When a certain kid asks you a question, you can tell sometimes no matter how you answer it, they want to hit you. It didn't take me long to figure out Mark Martinez always wants to hit everybody, but in the dark-dungeon tree house, they all seemed like they wanted to hit me. All except Camille. It's a good idea to have at least one good friend with you if you decide to go into a terrible place.

The teachers can't see in the dark part, underneath the tower jungle gym unless they come over and hunch down, which they never do. It smells like moss in there and pee. I don't know why I even went in. Recess was easier at my old school. It was on a big fenced-in slab of asphalt with cracks and weeds and old hopscotch markings, and one time a dead possum that was really dead and not just playing dead. You didn't have scary little places to make decisions about going inside.

"You can't be nothing. What are you? What are your parents?"

"Nothing."

"Maybe she's Catholic."

Camille Broderick's eyes seemed to sparkle in the light through the knothole, with dust floating in the stripe of it.

She nodded. She would never hit me because we're friends from the neighborhood.

"I guess so," I said.

"You can't just guess you're Catholic. That means you're Christian."

"OK," I said. I knew my parents wouldn't like me to just agree to be Christian like that because it's supposed to be a big decision – but of course they would want me to avoid a fight. Smart people always avoid fights.

"Maybe she's Methodist."

Camille hunched down and left. I watched her go, and counted the kids still in there with me. Seven. Mostly boys. To be honest, I was surprised she left. If it was a movie, I would have put one finger in the air as I saw her going, and called out, "oh!" to show her my dismay. "Dismay" means worry and disappointment all together. It's a pretty good word how it does both things. But I didn't call out or hold my finger up at all. I just stood there.

"Presbyterian!"

"Buddhist!"

"Jewish! No one's Jewish! Lutheran." They were all shouting and shoulder barging, but still no one actually touched me.

"What are you? What is she? What are you?"

I yelled, "Unitarian, Utilitarian, Hare Krishna, Ramadan!"

They were suddenly quiet. I knew they thought I was a weirdo, which can be helpful because then people leave you alone, but unhelpful because you don't always want to be alone, and you can't pick and choose.

"OK," I said.

"So what is it?"

"Just OK."

"That's no answer. You're asked a question, you have to answer."

They all still seemed mad, but some of the energy had

kind of drained away. Sarah Fitzgerald went out, and her bright red hair seemed to glow as she ducked down to get out into the sunshine. There was only one girl left, a girl whose name I didn't know. The rest were boys. Boys don't usually hit girls unless everyone is yelling and they get confused. Even if a bunch of boys get in a circle yelling fight-fight, you can tell, they still might not want to fight, they just want a teacher to come and break it up. They might throw a punch but their heart's not in it. The only boy who I thought would hit me for real because he hits everyone, including girls, which actually makes me kind of respect him in a weird way, was Mark Martinez. I knew he'd get in trouble if he hit me first, but I'd be in trouble too, maybe worse, once we'd have to tell what it was about. Mostly, I just didn't want to talk to my teachers about what I was or what I wasn't.

For some reason then most of the boys left. Like flies, buzzing off to some new mess somewhere else. The only two left in the dark-dungeon with me were Mark Martinez and Billy Whitaker. If they hit me and I yelled, people would think we were messing around even though I never yell because of the boy who cried wolf. I wondered if we could actually have a conversation, now that it was just the three of us, but they crossed their arms and turned their backs on me, blocking the door, so all I could do, really, was wait.

By the way, if you get a black eye, it's not really black, it's kind of purple. I never had a black eye or a bloody nose. My brother Chris has had both, but not from fighting. He gets bloody noses all the time. A lot of boys do, I think. If Mark Martinez hit me, I was going to hit him back. My fist got ready. And my lungs and my brain. That's probably all you need to punch someone's lights out – those three, fist, lungs and brain. I wondered if I hit him hard enough, I would break his nose.

Mark and Billy hunched over for a pow-wow, with their heads pulled low like turtles in their shells, and they put their arms over each other's shoulders, and they were whispering. I wished I could sneak around them and get out the little door. The beam of light from the knothole landed on the dirt floor between us. They stopped whispering and turned back around.

"You better think about it, Sandy Drue."

Billy pushed me hard, his grubby hand on my white dress in the middle of my chest, but I just stumbled back and didn't fall down. "Stay in here and figure it out, missy." I really wanted to hit Billy, I shifted my weight to my back foot to give it my all, but my left hand came to its senses, grabbed hold of the right arm and pinned it down, fist on wrist. I stood still. Mark laughed like it was the funniest thing he ever saw. And then he dragged Billy out through the little door, both of them laughing now, in their matching Toughskins with the yellow stitching, and I watched them go. I sat down in the dark then, on the cool dirt in my white dress and ponytail, and I could feel my heart beat begin to slow down a little, and then a little more as I sat there, breathing in the moss smell, not figuring anything out, not thinking about what they said or how much I'd wanted to hit them both, just thinking about the dirt floor and all the children's shoes that had stomped all over it over time and made it hard, until my heart beat slowed down to more or less normal, and I started to hear children shouting and running around outside, and birds and normal things, and finally the bell rang, and I hunched over and went out.

I thought when I was in there maybe Camille or someone would check on me, but I was kind of glad no one came back, because I wanted to be alone in there with that one beam of sunlight full of glitter. Also, I didn't think she was very nice to have left me in there in the first place. Even your best friends can get scared of a bully and not want to help you when the time comes. I wanted to just think about that for a minute too.

At home I asked my mom, "What am I?"

She said, "Tell them you're nothing."

"But what am I?"

She was making cinnamon rolls, and she stopped and clapped her hands over the sink and wiped her hands on the front of her pants. There was a little flour there, white finger prints on her black pants. Barley was watching her like maybe he would get a treat. He stays in the kitchen no matter what she's making, but he doesn't really care about cinnamon rolls. He'll eat bread if you give it to him, but you can tell he's not very impressed. Not as bad as grapes. He actually spits out grapes. Dog food you buy in the store is made mostly from potatoes, but mainly, dogs like meat. You can tell by the shape of their teeth. Fangs are canines. Dogs are canines. Police dogs are K-9s. So it all makes sense.

My mom looked at me for kind of a long time. "Sandy, you'll get to choose. You can choose anything you want to be. Anyone you want to marry."

"Like you and Dad?"

She squeezed my shoulder. "You'll make your own choices."

I was thinking I already know who I want to marry, even though he was absent today and wasn't in the dark-dungeon tree house. It's good he wasn't there. Some people believe a person can only have one true love their whole life. I don't know about that. But I think you can only have one true love at a time, like to marry them. Marriage love is different from other kinds of love. You can love a lot of people at the same time with the other kind of love, like your mom, dad, brothers, cousins, dogs and horses, and you can love books and movies and teacups and paintings, and you don't have to pick a favorite.

"They said I'm whatever my parents are. You're supposed to tell me."

Mom came down to my level to look at me more. "You get

to believe whatever you decide you believe. You can study everything people believe, everywhere in the whole world, and find out what you believe in your own heart for yourself. You can believe anything. It's all open to you. Everything."

She stood back up and put her hand on top of my head and squeezed and pulled me in close to her, my head against her hip, my ear against her stomach, and it smelled like cinnamon and butter and dough. Whenever people hug each other in our house, Barley tries to get in the middle. He nuzzled in between us, and I rubbed the furry place between his ears and my mom kept her hand there on my hair, warm and soft. And while she held her hand like that on my head, it seemed like it made sense, what she said, that there was no trouble whatever I would want to choose, and I didn't have to talk about it to anyone or go in the dark-dungeon ever again, and I could be nothing and anything and everything.

2. Avant-garde

om says I shouldn't use the word weirdo. The word to use is "avant-garde." Apparently in my adult life, I am going to learn how cool it is to be avant-garde. She's studying Jorge Luis Borges right now. He was an avant-garde South American writer who was also popular in Europe and the USA.

Avant-garde is the word for unique people, great artists, people who are brave and creative and interesting, and basically, the first ones to try a thing. Like pioneers, which most every American citizen respects, because the pioneers were so strong, they survived horrible winters and starvation and locusts and everything in the olden days. "Avant-garde" is the fancy French way to say "advance guard," which must be something military, since that word *guard* is in there. Why anybody would use a military term to talk about the arts makes no sense.

I really want to trust my mom, but I don't know. Maybe she's right that famous avant-garde artists today might have once been considered weirdos in their childhoods in the 40s or something. But no one can predict the future. If Jorge Luis Borges was a kid in my class at school now, I might not even like him. Mom might not like him either and wouldn't let him play at our house. Maybe by the time I'm a grown-up, there will be no such thing as avant-garde. Maybe I'll never be any kind of artist anyway, and I'll always just be a weirdo.

Still, I guess it's good if your mom thinks you're special

and there's a cool French word for what kind of special you are. If your mom doesn't think it, who will?

3. Barley's Ears

If someone asked me the best part of your dog I'd say two things. I'd say "all of him," and I'd also say "his ears." Barley has the best ears, the way they stick up when he's interested in something and he tips his head to the side, it's so cute. He has brown eyes. Sometimes he gets so happy when he jumps around wagging his tail so hard, it spins him in circles. Sometimes he gets so hyper that his ears flip inside out. But the soft fur right at the edges of his ears when he's just calm is my favorite. Also, his ears smell good, and when you rub them, sometimes he groans. "Mmrrrh, Mmrrrh." Especially if we've been out of town, like in Florida or California to see our grandparents, and right when he first sees us when we come back, that's when he really goes crazy. Maybe he gives up and he thinks we will never come back and bring him home again, so then when he sees us, he goes crazy with love. He stays in a nice kennel with nice dogs, but I think he likes to be home with us the most. Chris is the best at rubbing his ears. Also Barley does the most tricks for Chris, like play dead, sit, stay, lie down, roll-over, catch, beg, and shake hands. Sometimes when he gets really excited, he does all of his tricks in a row. His ears are the best, but sometimes his feet smell good too. Like grass and popcorn.

The reason I say "all of him" is because no matter if you're happy or sad or lonely or someone was mean to you, or you got a bad grade, or maybe you have something to celebrate, it's always better when Barley's there with you. Chris thinks so too, and of course my dad because he grew up with dogs, and he's the one mostly who taught Chris and me to teach Barley his tricks, but even my mom who grew up in New York and never had any pets loves Barley. Everybody needs someone to love and hug, and everyone loves and hugs Barley.

4. Don't Track Sand!

Sometimes I wonder if Barley gives up when he's at the kennel and thinks we're never coming back because maybe he gets a secret message that one of us was thinking we didn't want to go back home. Every big decision for a whole family must start with one person thinking or saying one small thing, and maybe dogs can sense that, even if they're not right there with you.

When we visit Grandma in Florida, my mom starts off the week just normal, but a few days into the trip, every single time, she starts saying she wants to stay there or she wishes we could all move back to New York and live in the same building like how she grew up. It's pretty weird, because she raises her voice at Grandma and vice-versa like they're sisters arguing about who got a stain on a skirt they share. As soon as they start, that's when Mom starts also saying she wants to live in that building. You moved my cross-word puzzle! Why did you have to clear up in here? You overcooked the pasta! We should have had take-out! The children are under my feet! Where's the Frisbee! You're wearing that? The table is sticky! Your grapefruit juice squirted everywhere! I've had it up to here with your children's things! Your juice! I don't even like grapefruits! When are you leaving? Go to the beach! Brush your daughter's hair! You forgot the Frisbee! Don't track sand!

They yell at each other about anything and everything. It's the weirdest thing. Maybe they are like sisters instead of mother-daughter because my grandpa died when my mom was just a girl and it was just the two of them in the apartment. But I'm glad Grandma doesn't yell at me that way, and I'm glad my mom doesn't usually yell at me that way. Even if she has the best Frisbee-throwing arm in the world and Chris and I always want to play with her, a grandma should act like a grandma, and a mom should act like a mom, and a daughter should not have to act like the mom, but should get to just be a girl. And when I'm a grown-up daughter, I hope if I overcook the pasta, my mom will be polite and just eat it and not make a big deal.

When they start yelling, Chris and I go in Grandma's bedroom and watch TV. Even though they're kind of yelling, you can tell they're not actually mad. I would much rather be with a person who raises their voice but isn't mad than someone who's really mad but stays quiet. You never know what's going on with a person like that. You only know eventually that person's going to explode.

5. The Perfect Hot Dog Hole

I better come clean. People mostly think I'm a nice girl. Mostly, I am. But what a person is *mostly* is not what a person is *always*, and you better know I'm not always nice. Everyone makes mistakes sometimes and does a mean thing by accident, but sometimes I am kind of mean even on purpose. You could ask Neal Berkley about it if you could find him. He could tell you about the other side of *mostly* and tell you what I did to him. Maybe he forgot by now, which would be good – for him and for me. I don't think anyone likes to remember the mean things they did to a kid in the neighborhood or in school or anywhere. Even if it was a really long time ago, like even more than a year. Let's see. I guess I was nine.

I'm the one who tricked Neal Berkley into the sewer and put the lid on, and I made my brother stand on top to keep him in. We were going to take turns keeping him locked in. That was my plan. Maybe no one needed to stand on the lid at night if Neal fell asleep in there, and anyway, I didn't know how we'd get out of the house without our parents knowing, for the night shift. And one other thing was what to do if it rained because then a sewer's dangerous. It's one thing to keep a kid down in the sewer when it's just a little mucky and dark and smells like metal. That's just mean. But making him stay down there in the rain is something else. Even just a little rain can turn into a flood that can kill people really fast. It seems weird, a "flash flood," like a flash bulb when you take a picture – that fast. Snap! Now the flash bar is hot, and the plastic's swollen like a hard blister and it stinks like burnt plastic because that's what it is. Less than one second, and it's over till you develop your film. Twenty-three people died in the Brush Creek flash flood. I can't explain how a flash flood happens, but I know you shouldn't go in the sewer when there's rain.

I planned to make him hot dogs. You just boil them in water – and we would poke them through the hole in the center of the sewer lid, so he wouldn't starve to death. My brother helped me get him in there, but I'm the one who planned it, and the person with the plan is always the worst person when people join together to do something mean. I was sorry Neal turned out to be so strong, after he finished whimpering like a baby, he just pushed the lid off, even with my brother on it, and scrambled out.

The problem with mean stuff is it can get out of hand. You might end up doing a lot more mean stuff than you really meant to. Especially if your friends are joining in and egging you on. Some people love to see their friends go past the boundaries and do awful stuff. But with Neal, it was really my idea, the whole thing. I think it's important I start with that confession, so you know I'm telling the truth. The first part of the truth is I'm not always nice.

When Neal poked a stick in the yellow jacket hole and they all flew out of the nest and he got stung seven times, mostly on his inner thigh, it wasn't me who'd dared him. I wasn't even there. I was inside reading *Are You There God, It's Me Margaret?* which is my favorite book of all times, even though the title seems too long, and approximately one-third of my friends aren't even allowed to read it because it's "controversial." Of course, that just makes me want to read it more... same for all my friends. My mom says it's good to read everything and be informed. I'm lucky to have the mom I do.

But that's how I know I wasn't there – because I was in my clubhouse reading. No one dared Neal to poke the yellow jackets. He did it on his own. Chris even warned him what that hole was.

The funny thing is his mom still let him play with us after the sewer, but after the yellow jackets, he wasn't allowed to play at our house anymore. Maybe he didn't tell her about the sewer until the yellow jackets, and that was the end of him playing with us. And then he moved away, and we never saw him again.

6. Hair

Last year we went to New York for Spring Break. It's a good time to go, if you're lucky with the weather. We were very lucky and had a nice clear day for the Easter Parade where everybody puts on crazy hats and feathers and costumes and marches down the road, some of them without even planning an interesting outfit. Spontaneity is the true beauty of New York. "Spontaneity" means anything can happen at the spur of the moment, usually good things, and they didn't need a lot of planning. Like someone in the parade might just be holding balloons or flowers or something. Or someone might build a paper mache model of the Sagrada Familia in Barcelona on their head and march along singing in Spanish. That lady's hat was my favorite. I'm going to go to Spain someday to see that cathedral in person if I can earn the money. There are a lot of steps there. I bet they warn you that if you go to the top you could have a heart attack. The Empire State Building and most cathedrals can give a person a heart attack. New York has my favorite cathedral I have seen in person so far, St. Patrick's Cathedral. I think I might like it enough to become Catholic. You can't get married in St. Patrick's Cathedral unless you're Catholic, and you can't just say you are for a day and then quit after your wedding. It has to be real and for the rest of your life.

We stood in the two-fer line, where you get two theater tickets for the price of one, although really they're just discounted, not actually two-for-one. My mom says that's the best place in New York to meet people. Chris and my dad went to the magic shop on 34th Street instead of coming with us to the two-fer line. I like magic tricks, but I don't like to know how they're done, or even what the packaging looks like when you buy your magic stuff, so I'd definitely rather do the two-fer line than Tannen's Magic, because then I can still be a good audience for Chris' magic tricks. If you know too much, you can't be astonished.

I love being astonished! You can't fake it, because astonishment is a sudden reaction and if someone tries to fake it, they are just a huge horrible faker, even if they mean well. It has to be real. With Chris' magic tricks, people are always really astonished, especially me. Chris loves that. Plus, the two-fer line is fun!

Mom started talking to the guy standing on line behind us, and it turned out he's a writer, so she told him I'm a writer too – or I'm planning to be. She knows I keep all my stories I type in a box, but she only reads them if I tell her it's OK, because she respects my privacy. She told that guy the thing I always want for Christmas is books on how to be a writer. By the way, in New York, people say you wait "on line" but most other places they say you wait "in line." I don't know why that is, but I know it's called "dialect," when the way you say stuff changes depending on where you're from.

I told the guy in the two-fer line I only have a manual typewriter at home, but I have electric typewriters to use at my dad's office. He said you don't need any typewriter. You can be a writer with only paper and a pencil – the equipment doesn't matter. The training matters. He asked me if I know about fiction, like what plot is, and setting, and dialogue, and conflict, and resolution, and I said I did, which is mostly true, although I'm not so sure about resolution. He had black hair and a navy blue pea coat and really cool glasses and a thick white scarf like a fishermen's knit sweater that he kept kind of grabbing and stroking like a cat and re-arranging it while he talked. I guess we were there in the two-fer line for about an hour, and he and my mom had a lot to talk about, which is also the beauty of New York. New friends are everywhere.

Now I kind of wish I hadn't said I knew all that stuff about conflict and resolution, because he might have taught me more. You never know where you're going to learn your most valuable lessons. He said your own creativity, commitment, and courage are what matter. Three C's. I memorized them as we were standing there in the cold. He went to Northwestern University when he was only in high school, where the student journalists also only have manual typewriters. My mom made a note, so I can go there in the future if I get accepted. You don't just get to go – you have to apply. Lots of things work like that, and you have to pay for them, unless you get a scholarship. It's important to keep trying if you don't get in at first, and don't give up even if you can't afford something. Then we got to the front of the line and bought tickets to the musical *Hair*.

I think it's good the tickets were half-price because in my opinion it was terrible. That was my opinion even before the whole cast came out at the end stark naked, which seemed really unnecessary. I would hate to be an actress in that show! I would refuse to do the grand finale. I think my parents were embarrassed that Chris and I were there to see all those actors and actresses stark naked on stage, with their tan lines showing and their hair, you know, on their bodies, and everything, which I guess was kind of the point. The men sure had a lot of dark hair down there. The whole private part of them was pretty dark, actually, I don't mean just the black guys who were kind of lucky because it didn't show so much since there wasn't so much contrast. The black ladies were lucky too, in that sense. I wouldn't be an actor or an actress in that show, no matter what color I was! I wonder if their singing changes when they're feeling awkward on the stage all naked. I'm not the best singer in the world any time, but I sure don't think being naked on stage would improve the situation.

The music in the show was pretty good though. I like the song "The Age of Aquarius." After the show, I was singing it day and night and driving my family crazy, even if sometimes they joined in. If my mom is actually mad, she says, "Sandy, I've had it up to here with you!" and then I know to stop. I should probably be embarrassed to sing out loud, but with my family, I'm usually not.

I think it's kind of funny that "bare" and "assed" are part of the word embarrassed. But we don't use the word "ass" in our family except for a donkey, and then, we mostly just say donkey.

My parents said they did the finale like that in the show because it was a challenge for the audience, and that's what art is. And when you talk about it like that, you capitalize Art and tell people you are capitalizing it. You say, "Art with a capital A." I thought that show was Art with a capital Awful.

7. Your Mother's the Most Beautiful Woman

This story is from the summer after that trip to New York when I was ten, but it sort of fits here. Anyway, writing a book isn't like a jigsaw puzzle with right-or-wrong pieces that can only fit one way.

There was a lady at the pool with orange-pearl fingernails. She had bright orange swirly-glittery nail polish painted on thick, like special paint for a car with rust. She must have done a lot of layers. I've never seen that lady there before. I kind of hope she comes back, but she might not be a member. Chris says he didn't notice her which is probably true because I don't think boys see really noticcablc ladies like grown men probably do. She wasn't talking to anyone. There were no grown men at the pool but if there were, I'm pretty sure they would have noticed her.

She was dark tan, darker than the Coppertone kid whose naked yellow behind is showing where the dog is pulling off her swim suit bottoms on their billboard. That's the worst ad. No one has yellow skin like that. It's sort of yellow like the inside of a peach. It's not skin! And no dog pulls off a girl's swimsuit. Dogs don't do that. And if a dog ever did, you would never take a picture of it happening and put it on your ad because that would be really embarrassing for the girl, and it's also rude. So even though I know that's not a photograph – it's an airbrush painting – that just makes it worse. Someone actually painted it to look like a real photograph. It's one thing to accidentally take a picture of something embarrassing or rude but then not show anyone, but it's really bad to make a picture like that on purpose and put it on a billboard. That Coppertone girl has pig-tails, so she is supposed to be cute. And dogs being silly are supposed to be cute. The whole ad is supposed to be cute. I hate that.

Also, Coppertone blocks out the sun on your skin and makes you NOT get tan, so what kind of stupid ad is that? My mom has suntan lotion that's supposed to make you tan, only it sort of makes you orange. Also, you can see the places where her hands rubbed it in.

The lady at the pool was tan all over, especially her hands, with those shiny orange fingernails. Also, she had puffy, big hair that was brown and gold streaked. I told my mom the lady was pretty.

As soon as I said it, I could tell by my mom's face, it was the wrong thing to say. Maybe that lady wasn't pretty at all, maybe I was wrong about the meaning of pretty. One time we were watching a movie from the 1940s and my mom said the actress had a good figure. I looked at the actress coming down the stairs all dancey step-by-step in her sequin swimsuit thing, with big feathers or angel wings or something, and her legs I guess in pantyhose but they might as well have been naked legs. I tried to memorize what it looked like to have a good figure. Far as I can tell, a person either gets one or they don't. I mean, you can't have a good figure if you get too fat or too skinny or if you walk with your shoulders hunched over and have bad posture. But other than that, it seems like having a good figure isn't really up to you. Anyone can walk down the stairs like they're dancing. So maybe her telling me that actress had a good figure wasn't a lesson for me to learn, it was just an opinion. I guess I hope I'll have a good figure in the future, but if it's just the luck of the draw, who knows? Maybe the lesson is you should go ahead and dance down the steps whatever you look like, and if you're enjoying yourself, that's probably way better than being boring with a good figure.

But I still kept thinking about that lady's orange fingernails, and I wanted mine the same. My mother said no, that lady had fingernail polish all the way to the sides of her fingernails. You should always leave the edges and the cuticle unpainted so your nails look longer. And you should use a neutral color. That is something you should know about being pretty. There are tricks to make your fingernails seem longer, and also your legs. You can wear beige shoes that match your legs, and it makes them seem longer. And your belt should match your pants. Also, she said, that orange was atrocious.

"OK," I said.

The weird thing is my dad suddenly said if you want to know about beauty, there is no one who knows more than your mother. She's the most beautiful woman in the world.

I don't know if that's true. Not all the kids at school think my mom's the prettiest mom in our class, even. But it seems pretty cool to have your dad think so. Obviously not everyone's mom can be the prettiest in the world, but everyone's dad can believe their own wife is the prettiest in the world. Maybe they just shouldn't tell other dads about it or there might be some fights.

8. Christmas Tree Whizzer

Twice a week my brother has soccer practice at the high school's football field that is all patchy with weeds. It's next to a big road with yellow lines, and when he's there, I wait on the side with my mom or sometimes in the car. There aren't any bleachers so we sit on the ground, against a chain-link fence when we sit outside. Usually, I like to go and watch. Usually no one notices me there, or sometimes one or two boys will say hi.

Chris has fifteen boys on his team, and you need at least eleven. I know all those boys, except sometimes if I'm cheering for them, I can't tell Kirk Kirby and Bill Gustave apart, because they both have blond hair and they both play fullback and they both are pretty fast, although I think Bill might be faster.

You can be fast even if you're short. My mom says those guys are scrappy. They both go for the ball and get it when other guys would give up. My dad says another good word for the way they play is "tenacious." You can remember that because if you really try hard for something, and you don't give up, you probably are at least ten years old. Ten for tenacious. Also, in French, they say *tenir* for "hold," and I picture a hand taking hold, like a tenacious fist that won't let go. It's probably the same word back in ancient Latin or Greek that made *tenir* in France and tenacious in England. People think having all different languages in the world makes it hard for people to communicate, but if you think about it, it also gives us something pretty amazing to discover when we realize no matter how different we seem at first, our roots are all growing from the same place. I love words! *Palabras*. The Spanish word for words is my favorite. The Spanish word for questions is pretty great too. *Preguntas*.

But between scrappy and tenacious, I'd rather be called scrappy. I mean in life. I'm not a soccer player. Girls don't play soccer. They should though, because I can head the ball, and I'm pretty fast, and I can dribble, and I know how to kick. Never kick from the tip of your toe or you'll have no control. If I could play, people might say "she plays like a girl," but hopefully, they'd actually think I play like a player. But that's not how things are. If I want to play a sport in high school, it will have to be field hockey in a plaid skirt. If I ever get to play hockey, put me in a rink in pads and skates and all the equipment, and ice-swipe sounds, and the flat stick, and puck, and thwacks in the cold.

"Thwack!" Six letters on a piece of paper, and you say it out loud and actually hear what it sounds like. That's called "onomatopoeia," which is another neat word to know if you want to be a writer. In *My Antonia* the grass goes "swish, swish," and that was my first onomatopoeia I learned. *My Antonia* is a prairie book by Willa Cather, and the locusts come and everybody dies and people freeze to death. It doesn't have anything to do with society today, so I didn't like it. Teachers are always making people read books that have nothing to do with real life today, but we all have to pretend they do.

Kirk Kirby and Bill Gustave look alike on the soccer field, but their personalities are really different. Kirk is mean. He punched Chris at the picnic last year. Sometimes if it's one of those two guys with the ball, I just yell "go!" even though if I knew for sure it was Bill, I would yell his name because he's nice to Chris, and sometimes we play at his house. When someone gets close to the goal, my mom always yells "shoot it!" She was a cheerleader in high school. She cheered in Madison Square Garden.

My dad says those boys are playing magnet ball and they need to keep to their positions. My brother is the goalie, so he doesn't get to shoot unless it's penalties, and then he's really good. But they don't usually do penalty shoot-outs under ten. But he makes good saves in goal, and that's important. My mom and dad always yell "good save!"

On Tuesday we were at Chris' practice, and I was mad because I didn't like my shirt that I had to wear. Mom says fashion sometimes requires a risk, but I think if it's between a mom and her daughter, and the mom is saying take the risk, the daughter should get to say no. It buttons at the back, at the top, but that's the only button, so otherwise it was open. She also says a girl's clothing speaks for her, and if that's true, then I think that shirt might say something I don't want to say about myself. Some girls my age already wear a bra – some girls even wear a bra at age ten. I don't think a girl my age should wear a shirt that tells everybody whether or not she wears a bra and makes them think about that question. So I sat against the chain link fence and let the metal dig into my back, to keep the gap in the back of the shirt closed.

All the boys were running zigzag drills so I'm sure they didn't notice me or my shirt. But then my mom said the boys all liked me. Like all fifteen boys, which obviously isn't true. That's ridiculous. She smiled like she was giving me a gift, even if it was a lie. Maybe it was a white lie. But it didn't make me happy because my back hurt from the fence and I wasn't going to move no matter what, and I didn't want any boys to like me or notice me at all. Boy, I hate that shirt. I wished she hadn't made me wear it on a soccer day.

We heard a car screech, loud and really long. We had time to turn our heads to the road and see a boy's body, in jeans and a blue t-shirt, navy blue, as his gangly body all arms and legs, just like it cart-wheeled onto a brown car's hood and windshield and then the car was stopped, and the boy's body bounced right off the windshield and back down over the hood, then, and it landed in the road where his bike had skittered over and was lying there. And other cars screeched too and stopped. I heard my mom shout "oh!" and I felt the fence dig into my naked back where I wanted it to stay and I felt her bony hand on my hand, and I thought how weird that a boy's body would fly right up there onto that car, and then go down as if it had meant to do that.

And all the soccer player boys, my brother and his two coaches and all of them were running now toward the busy street, my mother up and grabbed me and all the cars were stopped so no traffic would hit the boy, the bike, the brown car, and its lady or all my brother's friends streaming toward the road in their soccer cleats. The head coach, Mr. Dean, held them back, and the boy with the blue jeans and the blue t-shirt, who got hit by the car, he just stood up, like it was normal. He wiped his nose the way a boy does when wants to seem tough, with his arm. The other coach, Mr. Spalding, was on his knees then, looking at the boy, and when he put his hand on the boy's shoulder, the boy yanked his shoulder away, so I didn't think he was hurt. Just his feelings.

The lady in the car was crying though, pretty loud, and my mom put her hand on the lady's shoulder through the window. "You couldn't see him," my mother said. "He came out of nowhere. He's OK. The boy's OK." The lady cried more, and my mom gave her a Kleenex from her purse, all crunched up like it was used, only I knew it must be clean. And the lady held it in her hand and kept repeating what my mom said. "He came out of nowhere." Her windshield was cracked. You could still see through it, so she could still drive her car, but my mom reached in and turned off the lady's engine. She put her hand on the lady's back and kept it there. The boy stepped away from Mr. Spalding and stood kind of near me. He was taller than me. I knew him. His name's

Larry. I don't know how I knew his name.

I knew him from the Christmas tree lot that opens after Thanksgiving at the church down the road. He doesn't work there really, he only hangs around and sometimes he drags people's trees to their cars and asks for tips, even though the trees are supposed to be sold by boy scouts who would never ask for tips. He was there last year.

"You'll need to get checked by a doctor." Mr. Spalding tipped the bike back up and wheeled it to the sidewalk. He flipped the kickstand and left it there. The lady in the car was crying so much she couldn't breathe. I could feel the back of my shirt gap open and I wished it wouldn't. I tried to open my shoulders, like if I had really good posture to make the shirt close, but that seemed like a terrible way to stand in the road, with my shoulders wide open, like I was proud of something.

I could hear a siren coming toward us, maybe from near Brookside. Mr. Spalding kneeled down in front of him, but Larry jerked away and said, "I'm fine." Then he scuttled over to his bike, got on and raced away. It didn't even wobble. Both coaches started to run after him while the siren came closer, but then Mr. Dean came right back and made all the soccer boys go back behind the fence. Mr. Spalding must have chased Larry a block or two and then gave up, because he came panting back, same time as an ambulance arrived. I don't think Mr. Spalding normally likes to run.

The ambulance man took a look at the crying lady, mostly at her eyes, and she was only sniveling now, and nodding her head at my mom. People said that boy was lucky. Some of my brother's friends knew his family so they were going to call his mom. And my mom talked to the ambulance man, and I started not to care so much about my stupid shirt. That night at dinner, my mom told our dad about what happened and she said that accident will haunt that lady all her life. I think because she said that, now that boy Larry and his bike and that lady will haunt me all my life too.

Last year, when my mom and dad were picking out a Christmas tree that boy Larry told me he whizzed on all the trees. He said piss is good for Christmas trees, which isn't true, and also it is very rude to call it piss. In our house we only call it whiz, or sometimes pee, if someone doesn't know what whiz is. If a dog pees on grass too many times, it kills the grass, so obviously, it's not good for a tree. Especially one you've already chopped down.

Luckily my parents didn't buy a tree from that lot. We already have a silver store-bought fake tree with blue satin ornaments, and we add some ornaments Chris and I made at school. The blue balls are wrapped in satin threads and if you nudge them with your fingernail, you can see the white ball underneath. I don't like those blue balls even though they're very soft and shiny. I don't like the way those blue threads nudge and show the white. My mom calls it angel's hair. No one else has a silver tree, but at least our silver tree doesn't smell like pee.

Here's something weird. I felt kind of bad because I felt kind of good about Larry getting hit by the car. I'm glad he didn't die, but I hoped at least he got some bruises. Camille said if I went to confession, I would have to confess it because you can't be happy when someone gets hit by a car, even if you don't like him. That's one way to know you have to confess a thing – when you feel kind of bad about it. My mom says a person doesn't need confession to know what's right and wrong. It would be better if people knew on their own when a thing is bad, and if they're sorry they should say so, and they shouldn't have to double check everything with a priest. We should just know that stuff ourselves.

9. Equipment

I'm pretty sure everyone in the whole world my age knows the word "equipment," as in hockey equipment, including Lizzie. Joy and Lizzie are both my best friends, but yesterday I felt like only Joy could be my best friend from now on. We were doing spelling drills where you had to spell the word Mrs. Cope said and use it in a sentence, and Lizzie got stuck on equipment.

I would never say a mean thing about a person who got stuck on any word ever, except for one reason, even if I thought it was an easy word like cat, because who knows, maybe you have dyslexia or you come from another country where they don't call it a cat, or you confuse your c's and your k's or some other perfectly reasonable explanation. But the one thing I can't stand is if someone is a faker. Lizzie definitely knows the word equipment.

When she said she didn't know it, Mrs. Cope kind of stared at her like she was shocked, same as most of us, and then Lizzie did that thing with her eyes, like the girl cartoon skunk trying to attract Pepe Le Pew, where she bats her eyes and digs her chin into her own shoulder and holds a bouquet of cartoon flowers up against her chest and little red hearts fly out and circle around her head. It seemed really obvious Lizzie was trying to be cute, which made me feel kind of sick.

It's fine for a cartoon girl skunk to try to be like a person, exaggerated and silly, but a person shouldn't try to be like a cartoon. That makes no sense.

But it sure didn't seem to make Brian Fullerton sick. It seemed to make Brian Fullerton think Lizzie was extremely cute, and he wanted to help her sound out the word to spell it. His lips got all rubbery and slow. "E-quip-ment." Then the worst thing was that John wanted to help her think of what it meant, trying to help her remember where she might have heard it before. "In the gym… in the multipurpose room…" You might think the boys were just being nice, but when a girl's acting like a girl-skunk-cartoon on purpose, boys are never just being nice.

My mom says some boys like girls who seem weak or stupid. But I never thought John would be like that, and I never thought Lizzie would pretend to be like that. Equipment! It has three syllables and a "qu" in it. Really difficult!

And the thing is, Lizzie is already the prettiest girl in our class. She shouldn't have to act stupid to get attention.

Most kids say Brian's mother is the prettiest mother, because she looks like Farrah Fawcett in *Charlie's Angels* with her long jeans and streaky blond hair that flares out. I don't know if Brian's mother knows the word equipment or not. I mean, of course she knows it. I just don't know if she pretends not to know things so she'll seem cute. I'm glad I have a mom who would always want to be as smart as she possibly can. And I'm glad she found a husband who thinks that's how she should be.

10. Camille and Chocolate Soup

The way I first knew Camille and I would be friends was because we both had a white dress with a sailboat on it from Chocolate Soup and we both wore that dress on the same day, my first day of first grade, as a new girl in my new city. My dad says it was just a coincidence. "Don't read too much into it," he always says. But I think it means we are supposed to be friends, and Camille thinks so too, so that's good enough for us. If I didn't actually like her, then I wouldn't feel forced to be friends with her just because we had the same dress. Then it would just be a coincidence. That's how the world works. Now we've been friends in both schools, before and after the teacher's strike, I mean. It makes sense because we're neighbors too. The only difference is I have just one younger brother and she has two older sisters, and three older brothers, including the one who died in Vietnam. Also, I'm the oldest of the kids in my family and she's the youngest. And my dad's a businessman and her dad's already retired. Come to think of it, her dad fought in World War Two, and my dad was too young for that. But other than that, Camille and I are almost the same in every category.

The dress has a blue and red sailboat on the front, and a blue pin-dot sash. A sash is a fabric belt you tie in a bow instead of a buckle. The dress has red piping on the neck and arm holes. Chocolate Soup is expensive so my mom doesn't buy dresses for me there very often. Sometimes she sews dresses like the Chocolate Soup ones with fabric we pick out at Harper's Fabrics. Piping looks fancy but it's not that hard to do. It's just a little strip of fabric sewn into the seam. When you get right down to it, lots of things that look fancy are easy to do, and lots of things that seem easy are hard, even if you're very creative and a good artist. Mostly I like the dresses my mom makes. She says fashion should dare to take some risks.

One time Julie Fagan's dress split all the way down the side, not because of a fashion risk but just because the thread came out. She had to call her mom and go home. I felt sorry for her, but I don't think anyone saw what happened to her dress except me because I was sitting next to her. I didn't tell anyone about it because I thought it would be mean. Not even Camille, who would have loved a good laugh.

11. Red Cream Soda and the Ladies Room

P age and Annie and I snuck downstairs to the ladies room for grown-up ladies, in the church, by the Red Cream Soda machine. I wanted to go, even though they are best friends and if anyone was going to get in trouble, I knew two-against-one would mean the girl in trouble would be me.

If we don't forget our money on special Fridays, we are allowed to have a soda from the machine by the chapel, which is at the end of the hall by the ladies' bathroom. You can get any soda, but I always get Red Cream, and if they run out of Red Cream, I don't get a soda. Sometimes when I'm waiting my turn, I feel so desperate to get to the front, I imagine all the cars lining up for gas on the news. If you don't get there early enough, or you're just unlucky, you won't get any gas, and that's a real, true problem, worth showing on the news. If they can't get their gas tank filled up, they can't drive to the grocery store or the hospital or their jobs. I'm only waiting in line for a soda, but to me it's just as important!

I've never seen Red Cream Soda anywhere else. It really is bright red, in its glass bottle, when you hold it up to the sun in the window, and it tastes like bubbles and vanilla. And the bubbles kind of hurt your tongue and nose, just a little, and it might be weird, but I like that, just a little bit of hurting.

That's kind of an important part of why I like it so much. Not enough to make you sneeze.

My mom says it's not good for you, but I love it. Red Cream doesn't taste like cream. Mom says in New York they had Egg Creams, and that's a soda too, but it doesn't actually have an egg in it. It sounds as good as a Red Cream Soda. My dad says he's a fan of the Root Beer Float, which has ice cream in it, and it sounds good but really, it's disgusting. He had that on his first date, when he was nine at Friendly's Ice Cream Parlor in California. I sort of think he's making up a story there, because what boy goes on his first date at only nine? I might be in love with someone already, but I sure never went on any dates. By the way, people here call soda "pop," which is ridiculous.

Our whole class goes single-file down the back stairs, and since it's the back stairs you take to get there, Page and Annie and I knew we probably wouldn't get caught. Anyway, a person should be able to use whichever bathroom they want to use. It's a free country. Annie's got amazing gymnastic skills though, so she could probably hang from the walls in the bathroom stall for an hour or something, like in James Bond movies. But she'd probably just go ahead and get caught with Page and vice-versa, since I'd be the natural scapegoat. I used to think that word was "escape goat." I bet I'm not the only one.

One time on a special Friday I forgot my money, and there was a crate sitting right there with Red Cream Soda next to the machine. I thought I could take one Red Cream Soda from the crate and pay the money back later, like on Monday. It wasn't cold, the soda in the crate, but I figured it might even taste good warm. I didn't take it though. You can't borrow a thing or make a deal with someone to take a thing and pay back later when the other person doesn't even know. I had a sip of Page's, nice and cold from the machine. Just a sip, which made me sad because then I wanted more, but at least

I didn't steal it. Borrowing without making an agreement is the same as stealing.

So, Page and Annie and I snuck down the back stairs and went in that bathroom because we wanted to see if one of the church ladies had her period. Annie's mom forbids her from reading Judy Blume and any other "mature" books, so she especially wanted to go downstairs to that ladies room. I mean, maybe some moms don't want their daughter to read *Forever*, because it's about sex, but it's actually really good for our education and a very good book. But to forbid *Are You There God It's Me Margaret* makes no sense at all. Fine if you don't think a teenage girl needs to know about sex and birth control and stuff, but let's face it, we are all going to get our periods, and a good book about it would only help. No wonder Annie's so hyper and always curious about things. It can't all just come from her gymnastics, all that energy and eager stuff.

Anyway, there was the little white metal trashcan that looks like a house with a swinging lid roof that says PUSH. It goes between two stalls, exactly under the dividing wall, so two ladies having their periods would both have to use it, one pushing from her side, the other pushing the roof from the other. They can't push at the same time, or the lid won't open. I never want to need the trashcan house when someone else is in the bathroom next to me. I don't really like to go to the bathroom in a stall next to someone else in her own stall, but at big places like stadiums and hockey games, you just have to get on with it.

The lid screeched when we pushed it open. There was something white in there. We stayed as still and quiet as we could, hardly breathing at all. I wondered if I should go back upstairs alone before we took the thing out of the little house, but then all three of us were starting to shake, trying not to laugh, and it seemed fun. Also, looking at that lady's sanitary napkin would be important for our education, including

Page's and mine, and we've both read every single thing Judy Blume has ever written – some stuff twice.

The sanitary pad was all wrapped up in toilet paper, and it smelled like baby powder. We unwrapped it to see the blood. There was an awful lot of cotton for just a little blood. It seemed very wasteful. It's important not to waste things. In between Saturday cartoons, you see Smokey the Bear say "only you can prevent forest fires!" The Smokey the Bear song has been around since the olden days. Also, everyone knows, you should never be a litter-bug, and don't waste things! Maybe that's why some people have a lot of babies. When you're having a baby, you don't get your period and have to use up all that cotton.

I don't really want to ever get my period, but if you don't, you can't have kids. Every time my mom's really mad, so mad she says "I could just smash you," and then (when she calms down), she says, "Just wait till you have kids of your own," I think well, maybe I don't want kids. But every time I say that out loud, some grown-up always says, "Oh, honey, you don't have to decide that now," or "Sometimes that decision isn't ours to make," or sometimes they just say, "Well, now, that would be a shame."

12. The Olden Days

If you are talking about the olden days or asking questions about something that happened in the olden days, a grown-up might ask you, "What do you mean the olden days?" You should know what you mean when you talk about a thing.

The "olden days" is when your parents were kids or your grandparents, but no farther back than that. Men might have worn knickers and long socks with diamond shapes, and kids might have played with sticks and metal hoops instead of toys like we have today. I think everyone had an English accent, even if it was kind of fake, but I don't know that for sure because they didn't have tape recorders then, so how would we really know?

13. Magic Carpet Ride

My dad is a magician. He was a boy magician, and now he's a business man, but he still has a trunk full of magic things like a zippered banana and flowers that come out of a hat and a yellow plaid suit that smells like a thrift store. He might not still fit into it because he wore it in college. He paid his way through college with his magic and a scholarship. I sometimes tell people I know magic too, and when they believe me, sometimes I believe it too. That's a funny thing about believing something. How you know you made it up, but then even you believe it. It helps that Chris is a magician now too, even though he only does tricks for friends, and not big shows like my dad did. I can't actually do any tricks, but I have a creative imagination which is a different kind of magic.

I told Lizzie I could make the purple flower bed turn into a magic carpet and fly us above the city, and I'm pretty sure we both believed it. We had already spent the morning with a police radio her dad got at an auction, and we were hiding in the bushes and shaking the branches and telling a man on the radio there was a tornado until Lizzie's dad caught us and made us go to the police station and apologize. He didn't think the radio worked, but for some reason it worked for us, which already seemed like magic.

Then in the afternoon we chipped fossils out of her stone pillars, which also seemed like magic, that a million-year-old fish could be there, its bones right there in that rock, or a shell, or an ancient bug in her stone pillar, for a girl to chip out with a hammer and a kitchen knife and stick it in her pocket. Also, Lizzie takes ballet with me, and piano lessons from the same lady, who makes us clip our fingernails if she hears them click on the piano keys and makes us go to the symphony four times a season, and you have to wear tights to the symphony. Not the same tights you wear for ballet of course. At the symphony you have to wear tights for getting dressed up, red or blue or green – not pink ballet tights with seams. The four times you go to the symphony can't include the Lollipop concert that we go to with school.

Three years ago, when it was the Lollipop Concert, I had my hockey puck with me, my prized possession that the Scouts manager gave me for being their number one fan, which I was then and still am. I was bored in there in the dark and holding my puck in my lap, and I dropped it. It rolled away in the theatre full of school children, and my teacher wouldn't let me stay after and look for it because our whole bus would have had to wait. I didn't cry but I was extremely sad. She said that would teach me not to bring out something I love, if I can't risk losing it. And that made me even more sad.

My parents say the word "priceless" is when something means so much to you that no price would ever be high enough for it. My hockey puck was priceless. I'm sad I don't have it anymore, but I'm kind of happy at least I played with it instead of hiding it away and maybe forgetting about it. If something's priceless I think you should be careful with it, but you should still play with it, just not in a dark theatre with a slanted roll-away floor. Otherwise, why have it? Maybe you are someone who should have just nice things, or even very nice things, but not priceless.

But back to the magic carpet. Lizzie knows my dad was a magician. She said she believed I could make the flower bed lift up and fly, and even though it never did, she sat out there in the purple flowers with me long enough that I knew she believed me. It's probably good it didn't work because that would have been scary, since a carpet doesn't have any handles, and neither do flowers, and what if it went fast and high and far away? How would we ever get home? But Lizzie didn't care about any of that, and we weren't scared – we were just there with our fossils in our pockets, believing. That's a good friend – not just good, not just very good – but a priceless friend, and now she will be my friend forever, no matter what.

14. Cleats

Yesterday Kirk Kirby tripped Chris and kicked him when he was down, and then he stomped on his shoulder. He said it was an accident when they yelled at him, but everyone knew it was on purpose. His cleats made purple dots bruise in a pattern on Chris' chest. I hate Kirk Kirby. Chris never did anything mean to Kirk. I think some of the other boys hate him too because they told Chris afterwards, even though no one said anything to Kirk at the time, which just proves that boys are like sheep.

At dinner, my dad said he's going to talk to Mr. Dean and Kirk's parents, which seems like a good idea. My mom was in Chris' bedroom last night though, and I could hear her talking to Chris even though she was talking quietly. She said, "Punch his lights out."

I held my breath so I could hear better. I was in the bathroom between our rooms and I held my toothbrush very still.

She said every group of kids has a bully, and every group has a victim. Kids in classrooms, Sunday school, baseball or soccer or swim teams, that's just how it is. You punch that kid, and show them all you're not their victim.

I wanted to ask how hard, and what if you miss, and what if he punches you back and makes you bleed, and isn't violence supposed to never be the answer, but then I'd have had to come out of the bathroom, and they'd know I was listening to their private conversation. So I had to just think about it on my own, and I decided she might be right. Even if Kirk punches him back, at least those boys will see Chris isn't afraid. I want to hit him too, but that probably wouldn't help Chris.

They let Barley sleep in Chris' bed last night, which was probably nice for both of them even if Barley was back downstairs in his own bed in the morning.

15. Lanyard

Most people are really thinking about crafts when they pick Arts and Crafts for an activity at summer camp, but in my family, we usually go past following instructions to make a thing anybody and everybody can make, so we're not just craft people, we're artists.

Chris and I both pick Arts and Crafts mostly for the leather wristbands. You can stamp your initials and butterflies and flowers in the leather, and dye it dark if you like. Last summer I even made a belt and Chris made me a buckle for it in silver smithing. It's my prized possession from last summer. Maybe the belt is a craft and not really an art, but the buckle is definitely art.

For Mom's birthday, he made her a lanyard keychain with pink and blue plastic lanyard strings. They take forever, and you end up with a weird braided stick of colored plastic on a key ring that only a mom would probably want, but since Chris is kind of an artist, he made his lanyard fancy. It had figure-eight parts and special knots and it took him almost all week to do it. It was pretty cool.

But then this boy named Van took it. He said he found it in the stable, but I think Van took it from the art room. But Van and Chris and I were in the corral, not on our horses yet because we were waiting for horse assignments, so we were just there in the corral. Van held up Chris' lanyard he made for our mom and started saying "Piss, is this yours? Piss!"

I get it that piss and Chris rhyme, but come on, have a little imagination! Only the most pathetic people in the world ever use that one. A good insult, if it's imaginative, can be pretty satisfying. But then Van held up Chris' lanyard over a horse puddle and he said, "Bombs away!" and he dropped it in the pee.

I saw Chris' face, and it's like I felt every single thing he was probably feeling, only more. That was his *art*. It came from his own creative self with those fancy loops he invented. And it was for our mom. Every artist has to be very brave to put their own creative self out into the world in their creations, and Chris does that. He put it in that lanyard he made for our mom. And I think a lot of artists do their best things when it's for someone they love. That idiotic boy Van probably couldn't have even imagined how important another kid's lanyard might be. Chris ran over and slugged Van, and I plucked the lanyard out of the puddle, which wasn't really that gross, but I was still feeling like I was either going to cry or throw up. I didn't want to do either one, so I slugged Van too after Chris did, and I yelled at him not to mess with us. I only got him in the back, and he probably didn't feel it at all, but it was better than nothing. Chris and I didn't get in trouble because all the witnesses said Van started it. But none of us got to ride that day, and we still had to groom our horses and muck out stables, Chris and Van and me, as if we were old friends. More proof that life isn't fair. At least Mom loved the lanyard, once it was clean.

16. Little Statues, Little Dog

Barley is a medium-big dog, but he's always nice to people and other dogs. It's funny how sometimes little dogs are mean to big dogs, barking with their high-pitched yapping and snarling at them like they think they're tough and scary, and the big dogs just look at them like "you're a silly little thing," or "you are really annoying, and I've had it up to here with you." I guess that's the same with people, actually. Small people sometimes get all feisty around someone big and powerful, and it's so dumb because all they do is annoy everyone.

There used to be a boy named Andrew who lived around the block, where no other kids live. His mom wouldn't let us play inside. Their house wasn't very big, but it had a lot of delicate things in it with gold paint decorations. Like little old-fashioned statues and bells, you know, porcelain with flowers, and their carpet was beige and smelled like old ladies. I guess his mom thought we might break something even if we never went in the room with the delicate things. I never saw his dad.

Andrew had black wooly hair, he wasn't very tall, and he had a little white dog with very soft fur and pink skin, and you could feel its bones. Like an old grandma, but not a nice one, with that pink skin underneath, and small and bony. Andrew told Chris and me we were bad because we didn't know what a sin was. A sin is a bad thing you do. Not just bad but really bad, and God gets angry. It's a sin to not know what a sin is.

He didn't have any fun things to do in his yard and I thought his dog was more like a cat, a mean skinny one, like the kind of cat you never want to touch.

Cats are weird but they're always thinking, you can tell, and I think that's neat. But Andrew's dog was like a cat with no thinking, and I didn't get how it could be a sin not to know the word sin. It's not like words just come into your brain on their own, so if it's a sin not to know it, well, that's someone else's sin for not teaching it. And if the grown-up never knew it was a sin to not teach it, then you can't blame them either. The whole idea of sin seems silly.

I didn't like playing at Andrew's house, and I wouldn't even tell you about him, but here's what happened. Phyllis' big black dog attacked Andrew's old bony cat-dog, and even though everyone said leave them, they're dogs, they're just playing, never get in the middle of it, it didn't look like playing, and I heard later that Andrew's dog died. Andrew wasn't there at Phyllis' house – just his dog was, for some reason – so at least he didn't see it when it happened, but it's still awful and sad. I don't know if dogs commit sins, but I think Phyllis' dog killing Andrew's dog should be a sin. It makes me pretty sad to think about it even now and it happened like three years ago when I was about eight and first started writing my stories. After that, Andrew moved away with all those little statues.

17. Fireflies and the Sprinkler

There are three pages that have been there in my box full of stories, stapled together and lying there like a sleeping rattle snake. Every time I rummage through, I'm careful not to touch it, like I don't want to wake it up. Maybe it would have been better not to even write it down. I haven't talked to my mom about it or Chris or anyone. But if a thing gets stuck in your mind and bothers you, you might feel better if you write it down. It puts the words on paper and keeps them there so you don't have to keep remembering it.

Maybe it didn't even bother Lizzie and Maggie and Jennifer at all, which actually would kind of make it worse for me, like the rattle snake is extra poisonous. Baby rattle snakes have the strongest venom. Don't think that since they're small or young they're not the dangerous ones.

But I know real writers have to put stuff in their books they'd rather not talk about. The problem with being brave though is once you're brave one time, you might have to keep on being brave whether or not you still feel like it. You might wish you'd realized you're actually kind of a weak person from the start. But it would be terrible to look back at a time you had a choice and know you chose to give in and be weak just because you were afraid in the future it might be hard to be brave. That's not just weak, that's a coward. So it's best to be brave the first time, and then accept the fact that you're going to have to just be brave from then on.

The thing from Lizzie's house was two years ago. I was the oldest. I was eleven. Lizzie was still ten. Maggie was nine, and Jennifer was eight or nine. But the point is I was the oldest, except for Lizzie's parents. But when you're in a group, the oldest isn't always your best leader.

It's kind of weird to read it now, from my younger self, especially how it ends, because like I said, I haven't talked about it.

Anyway, here it is:

Uncle Ned isn't even Lizzie's uncle at all, he's a friend of her dad's, and maybe not a very good friend, because Lizzie had never even met him. He is bald-headed on top and the rest of his hair is scrawny-curly, an in-between color like rat-brown plus mouse-gray, and it touches his shoulders and puffs out when he walks. He's Mr. Hardmann's fraternity brother and he was driving cross country so he came to stay. He's from Hollywood and he makes movies, and the weird thing was how much Lizzie's dad was laughing at everything Uncle Ned would say until suddenly he stopped laughing and got so sleepy he had to lie on the couch, and he didn't get up the whole rest of the time.

It was really hot, but for some reason they didn't have the air-conditioning on – just the windows and the back door open so we could hear the cicadas, which Uncle Ned said really freaked him out. "They're really freaking me out, man," he kept saying, and Lizzie's parents would repeat it and laugh. I love the sound of cicadas, especially when they really start whirring, and I don't know why Uncle Ned was so freaked out. Also, I don't know why we all had to call him Uncle Ned when he isn't even Lizzie and Maggie's uncle. You can call cicadas "katy-dids" if you want. There's an old wives' tale that every seven years they go through cycles where they'll be extra loud all summer. A lot of old wives' tales turn out to be true.

And I thought it was also weird that we all had to sit at the table because we all have long brown hair and he wanted to brush it for us. I don't know any men who like to brush girls' hair, and that's what was freaking me out, man. He was brushing Jennifer's hair, and Lizzie and Maggie sat on their parents' laps and Uncle Ned said he would do mine next, so I said no, thank you, I already brushed my own hair today. I could see the fireflies in their back yard through the screen door, and I wanted to run outside. Lizzie's mom didn't even have a brush, she was just petting Maggie's hair with her hand, like a dog and raking her hair with her fingertips. And then she stopped and held up her iced tea to her cheek and her neck and said how hot it was. She wasn't lying either. They could have at least had a fan on if they didn't want to use the air-conditioning.

So finally we got to go outside and there were a million fireflies. I know some people will tell you they only come in yellow-green, but if you chase them all around through pine trees and oaks and elms in the park, and just in the yard, you'll see the other colors, like blue and purple and even pink. You have to be very gentle when you catch them, just cup your hands as big as you can. And if you put them in a jar, be sure it has some leaves and twigs and air holes, and only keep it a little while. You might think you can keep a jar of fireflies as a night-light, but they won't keep lighting up very long, and in the morning they'll be dead and you'll wish you'd let them go before it was too late.

Lizzie's mom brought us the biggest jar she had for making sun tea, all cleaned out, and she even popped holes in the lid with a nail, which my mom would never do because then of course you can't use it for iced tea again, but Mrs. Hardmann said it's good to be a little reckless in our youth. We all caught a lot of fireflies and put them in the jar, even Uncle Ned and Mrs. Hardmann. Probably 20 or 25 in there lighting up. And still, there were about a million minus 25 in the yard. Maggie caught the most, maybe then Lizzie, but we all caught a ton.

That part I liked much more than the dumb hair brushing at the kitchen table. Brushing your hair at the kitchen table is rude, anyway. Hair brushing is for bedrooms and bathrooms. Uncle Ned said his next movie with Kristy McNichol is about girls, so he wanted to make a study of our hair. He calls his movies films. Before Mr. Hardmann fell asleep, he told Uncle Ned he says "films" and "cinema" to sound important. I'm pretty sure Mr. Hardmann was making fun of Uncle Ned, but all the grown-ups laughed.

It was really hot and muggy, so Lizzie's mom turned on the sprinkler and everyone starting shouting and jumping over the sprinkler head. Mrs. Hardmann put the jar of fireflies in the house where the lights were all on, which I don't think was very good for fireflies who like the twilight. Running through the sprinklers is good if you're hot, but it's nowhere near as good as going to the pool. I had my red shorts and red and yellow striped halter top on, and I didn't mind if it got wet. We all were barefoot. But Uncle Ned came outside and said we should strip, which as you probably know means take off your clothes, and just like that, poof, Maggie was leaping around in the sprinkler naked. Maggie gets naked at the drop of a hat. But I looked at Lizzie and didn't think she wanted to strip, and I definitely didn't want to, and I don't know Jennifer that well, so I couldn't say about Jennifer, but then Uncle Ned was telling Mrs. Hardmann about the beauty of the female form at every age, and he wanted to capture all four of us with our long hair and our naked bodies in the sprinklers for his movie. Mrs. Hardmann stopped laughing for just a minute, but then she was back at it, like "oh, Ned, oh, ha ha," and I practically thought she wanted to be in his movie running through the sprinklers too. Maybe "movie" was the magic word because next thing I knew Lizzie and Jennifer were naked too, and I was still in my red shorts and halter top, all wet, and all our hair was stringy and stuck to our backs, and not floating in the air like he said he wanted it to. All their clothes were in a big wet ball of fabric near the door and you couldn't tell anymore whose was whose or what was what or what colors were even in the wet mess of clothes over there in the far shadow of the porch. I knew it had purple and blue and green and brown but it just seemed like an alien animal with wings and fangs and feet and claws and thigh muscles all tucked up in there, wet and powerful and ready to leap out and strike a person if they'd get too close.

He told us to lift our hair up into the air to try to make it fly. Also, he wanted the fireflies to be in the scene, but every idiot knows a firefly isn't going to run through a sprinkler any more than it's going to fly around lighting up the rain.

And he kept saying I had to hurry up because he was going to lose the light, and Mrs. Hardmann turned on the porch light for him, all gold and glowy, and he said it was good, but it made the moths come, and he still wanted me to be naked like the others. He started a stupid chant like at a baseball game , so they were all chanting and clapping at me: naked, naked, naked – even Mrs. Hardmann, laughing the whole time. I thought Mr. Hardmann would come outside and ask what was going on, but he never did.

And then Uncle Ned told us all to do gymnastics, so we were doing cartwheels over the sprinkler, and back bends and round-offs, especially the three who were naked, he said his camera loved the whole thing, but I know it was really him who loved the whole thing. Even me, even in my wet clothes, although he seemed to especially love the others, and he kept turning his camera to face them, one after the other, doing backbends. I don't think that's what love is at all. My mom says the words love and hate are overused, misused, and abused. Uncle Ned doesn't have a wife, so he probably doesn't even know what love is.

Then Mrs. Hardmann came out to the grass and got

in on the act, leaping over the fanned out water jets like a ballerina in her dress. She did a handstand, which I've never seen before – I mean, I have never seen anyone's mom do a handstand or any kind of gymnastics, in any kind of outfit. She held it pretty long. Her arms must be strong. Her legs seemed really long. The porchlight was like a golden triangle fanning out over the green grass, with Lizzie's mom in the middle of it, shrieking and laughing and upside down as the water jetted back and forth. Of course, her dress flew up to her head, and she was all wet, and her underwear showed white like it was glowing. I could even see the dark part through her underpants. I don't know. Maybe it was a shadow. Maybe it was my imagination. But I didn't think I should see that part of Mrs. Hardmann, and I didn't think a mom should be doing that at all. Shadows and imagination can get a person into trouble that never would have existed if the person hadn't let their imagination run away with them. But the whole thing made me uncomfortable.

You have three choices when you're uncomfortable: 1) you can tell yourself to get over it, there's probably nothing wrong, or 2) you can do something assertive to stop the problem, which usually means saying something very firmly like a reprimand, which is definitely hard to do when the problem is coming mostly from a grown-up like a teacher or your friend's mother, or 3) you can set aside the question of whether it's actually a real problem or not a real problem and just accept the fact that it's a problem for you, and you can leave. I didn't think I should see Mrs. Hardmann's underpants, and I didn't think a mom should be doing that with her daughters and their friends all around, and some man she barely knows and his movie camera.

I said I had a stomach ache, which wasn't a lie. I felt awful, and I had to go home. I went in the kitchen all wet, and I didn't worry about tracking in my cold footprints, even with little green grass clippings sticking to the Hardmann's white floor. I could hear Mr. Hardmann snoring on the couch in the living room, and I called my mom. That jar of fireflies was there on the kitchen table with the hairbrushes, and they were hardly lighting up, so I turned off the light in the kitchen and watched them to see if they'd light up again. But they were hardly moving or doing anything at all, which made my stomach ache worse.

Since my clothes were wet, I got my overnight bag and went in their downstairs bathroom and locked the door. I changed into my night gown, my purple flowered one with ruffles that goes all the way to the floor. It's my favorite nightgown, even if it was kind of too hot outside to wear that one. If they'd had on the air-conditioning, it would have been OK. I made my own decision about those fireflies, and I took the jar outside their front door, where I planned to wait for my mom, and I opened the lid and let them go. At first they didn't seem to want to go, and when they finally did, they didn't light up at first, but then they did, and I felt a little better. Plus, I was wearing my nice dry nightgown, only getting a little wet down my back from my hair. Sometimes when it's muggy, you actually feel better in long sleeves, if they fit loose, and as long as your clothes are cotton. I don't like sweaty skin or being sticky.

When I went back in the kitchen to put the jar back, Mrs. Hardmann was in there and made me come outside with them because it isn't safe for a girl to wait on someone's front porch all alone. And when I went outside, Uncle Ned had turned off his camera but everyone was still dancing naked over the sprinkler and he was clapping and singing. And suddenly a blue firefly, my favorite color firefly flew near him – they're very rare – and he reached out a hand and grabbed it. You should never catch a firefly with only one hand, even if you're a grown man and you have giant hands, because they need space and you have to be gentle. Uncle Ned grabbed Lizzie by the shoulder as she ran past in the slippery wet grass, and she was laughing and so was he, more like howling like a wolf, and he slapped his big hand onto her stomach with the firefly and smeared its light from her belly button to her hip. Even writing that down makes me almost cry. That blue firefly.

I could see her face in the porch light when she looked down at the smear of light on her stomach, and I don't think she thought it was one bit funny, but then she ran off to do another cartwheel, and I just stood there watching her bare feet and her gray-pink knees come around as she cartwheeled, and then I went inside to wait for my mom in the living room with Mr. Hardmann snoring.

I hate Uncle Ned, and I don't think I'm overusing the word. I don't care if Lizzie and Maggie and Jennifer all become movie stars, or Mrs. Hardmann for that matter, who I think was being a show-off. They'd probably all just say I was jealous. For the record, I wasn't jealous at all. I think I'll ask my mom her opinion about it. Although then she might not let me play at Lizzie's.

18. Books and the Beginning of *Jaws*

Scientists and doctors have a lot of stuff figured out about the human body, but sometimes a person also learns important things from reading fiction books. Like *Jaws*, for instance. I didn't read very much of it, it's still too grown-up for me, I guess, because I got bored in the first chapter, which must mean I'm too young and my brain is immature, but in the beginning there's this lady who goes swimming in the ocean, and it says the cold water is like a finger that goes up her vagina. Even though *Jaws* is written by a man named Peter Benchley, I figure Peter Benchley must have a sister or a wife or a lady who tells him pretty private stuff because that happens to me too – in the pool. I kind of wondered if it was normal or not, and reading *Jaws* made me realize it is. It's kind of like when you drink hot chocolate and you feel the warmth go down your esophagus. The human body seems pretty mysterious and then you feel the cold water come up into you or the hot chocolate go down into you, and it's like you kind of see inside yourself, and part of the mystery gets solved.

There's no reason to read the rest of *Jaws*, because the very next scene is ridiculous. Peter Benchley makes that lady get attacked and half-eaten by a shark, and the top half of her dead body washes up on the beach, and her boobs are deflated. Peter Benchley should have asked his sister or wife about boobs. They're not balloons that deflate when a shark's tooth pops them! As my mom would say, for goodness sakes, Peter Benchley! Grow up!

Thinking about that first part of the book *Jaws* though, (when the lady's still swimming), was another reason I didn't think a bunch of naked girls leaping around over a sprinkler at the Hardmanns' house was such a hot idea. Bad stuff can get in you if you're not careful.

19. Ginny and the Period Girls

Sometimes good information also comes from non-fiction books, which should be trustworthy because the publishers have fact-checkers to make sure everything's true. That's the difference between non-fiction and fiction, although you can learn plenty from fiction, even though it's not supposed to be true.

There's a little non-fiction booklet you have to write away for and get in the mail from the Tampax people that teaches girls about their periods. People call it their "change." And some people have goofy sayings for when it's happening, like "my red haired aunt is visiting." That would just be confusing in my house because Aunt Lula's hair is brown, unless she's being adventuresome, and then it's blond. But if something is supposed to be natural and you're not supposed to be embarrassed about it, you probably shouldn't have to use a saying or a secret code.

The booklet has pretty good information. Three girls in the booklet get their periods, and they're all pretty much the same age as my friends and me. One girl's name is Ginny, not Jenny, and it's not a typo. I think it's a cool name, and she's the popular one of the three girls. It matters a lot who is popular and who is not, even though everyone says it doesn't matter, or it shouldn't matter, but obviously it does. I am not very popular. But some people might think I am, it's all just a matter of perspective.

The booklet says some girls' boobs might not be the same size when they start to grow, but they might even out over time, like it's a race and the smaller one might catch up. Or it might not. You're not supposed to worry about it if your boobs are different sizes. I hope mine will be the same though, because I've noticed in JC Penney that they don't sell bras with two different size cups, so what are you supposed to do if you need two sizes for one person? Not everyone knows how to sew, and a bra seems pretty tough to make. Sewing elastic is tricky.

We don't call them boobs in our family, but every time someone says breasts, they sort of seem embarrassed, like it's not the right word either, so I'm sticking with boobs. Also, not everyone's hair down there comes out the same color as their hair on their head, and that doesn't mean anything. And some girls might experience an unpleasant discharge. Of course, it doesn't happen to Ginny because she's the popular one who only good things happen to and she can probably just waltz into any JC Penney and buy a bra right off the rack. I already know I'll probably get all the weird and rare and unpleasant stuff. At least now that I read that booklet though, I'll know I'm not the only one.

20. Squirrels and Trees

The thing about time is it's slippery. I've heard some people say elastic, which makes sense if you're measuring it by a long strip of fabric. Some time periods stretch out beyond what you'd expect they could, like when you do the three-minute wall sit for summer volleyball, and your legs feel like it's 15 minutes. But I don't think it's just elastic. It's more like rubber. It stretches like a rubber band, and springs back, but also it bounces all around – different ideas and memories, not in any sequence that makes sense or that you'd ever expect. Your brain jumps from one thing to another with no warning. So it's slippery and it's rubber. A greased Superball? There's probably the perfect metaphor out there, but I just can't find it yet.

Since Joy moved away I send her a lot of letters and ask questions, and then the soonest I'll get an answer is about two months later. By then I usually have forgotten the questions, so luckily Joy repeats the question when she answers it, so I remember. And of course, I try to do the same for her. I always have her letter on my lap desk when I write her back. Letter writing is an art. The separation is two things, really. Miles, for one, but also time. It's not like you can just keep a trail of all your letters going back and forth every time. Even if it's fun to imagine, that would take too much paper and cost too much postage.

I think the human brain is like a squirrel, how it runs all over a tree, up and down and branch to branch. But the squirrel always comes down with its treasures to bury them and keep them safe underground. No matter how scattered your ideas get in your brain, it's good to keep them safe in someplace grounded. That's a great word – "grounded." That's what sending letters to Joy and getting letters back from her does for me, when my brain is like a squirrel. It makes me feel like I have my feet solid on the ground, maybe even with a buried treasure tucked away at the root of my crazy squirrel tree.

21. Rules

Ding Dong Ditch 'em

1. Ring someone's front doorbell. (Don't choose the meanest neighbor you know).

2. Run away before they answer.

3. Important note: Do not hide, laughing, in bushes nearby or you'll get caught.

4. Second important note: Tell friends at school if you want, but never any adults in the neighborhood or you will get in trouble even if you didn't technically get caught!

Crank Calls

1. Choose any phone number from the white pages or from your head.

2. Important note: Be sure it's only seven numbers so it won't be long-distance.

3. Call the number. You and your friend can both be on the same phone, tilted sideways so you can both hear. Camille and I like her upstairs phone because it's green.

4. When a person answers, ask, "Is your refrigerator running?"

5. The man will say yes and then you say, "Then you better go catch it!"

6. Hang up and laugh.

7. Important note: Do not start laughing before you talk or that ruins it.

8. One option: You can say "Do you have Prince Albert in a Can?" which is old-fashioned tobacco in a red tin can, and if they say yes, you say, "Well you better let him out," like Prince Albert is a real man. I don't recommend this one though because no one has ever heard of Prince Albert in a Can unless they work in an antiques market, so it's not worth the effort. That's called Return on Investment. You get a better return if you invest your time in a refrigerator call.

Rate calls

1. Note, people can get their feelings hurt so be careful how you do this.

2. Make your list of girls the boy might like. Be sure the main one you want to know about is close to the middle, so he doesn't have to start there or end there. There's always a lot of pressure at the start, and also at the end, even if they don't technically know it's the end. Somehow they must sense it, like a dog.

3. If he has a friend over and you think the friend is on the other line, tell him no, only he can be on the line. It's best to do this in fifth or sixth grade, when boys and girls really kind of like each other.

4. So he answers and says hello, and you say, hello, will you accept a rate call? Usually you don't say who you are.

5. He might say no. That's just because he's never done one, or he is scared, or maybe he knows who you are and he likes you or he knows who's sleeping at your house tonight and he likes her or he doesn't like her... it could be anything. You can say OK and then call again and ask again later. Usually he will do it. If he really doesn't want to do it, he will make his mom answer the phone and say he can't talk. If he does that, you have to give up.

6. So in the case where he says yes, you say OK and the first girl, like: "Melissa" and maybe he'll say "five." So next you say "Constance" and maybe he'll say "five." And then you say "Sissy" and maybe he'll say "four."

7. Now you are figuring out his pattern. He doesn't want to be mean, but he really doesn't like Sissy, except of course maybe as a friend. Maybe that's because he knows Sissy likes him and he doesn't want to lead her on. So it might seem mean at first, that he only rates Sissy a four, but actually it's nice because he's not leading her on. Get it?

8. Then let's say you say "Annie," and it's Annie who is spending the night and she really likes him, so this is THE ONE. And he says six. Don't scream or act stupid and don't let Annie do that because that will ruin everything with him, and he won't even like her anymore. And even though you got your answer that he likes Annie, you have to do the rest of the names as if you care about them just as much. One time, we thought the six was the answer and then Wendy got an eight at the end which was not what I expected at all, and we only put Wendy in there because we ran out of names!

9. Important note: whatever you think you know about boys and who they like and why they like them, you

are probably wrong. There is just no benefit in trying to figure it out because you can only get so far. Also, whatever was true a week ago can change the next week, so feel free to do rate calls whenever you want.

10. Second important note: if your boy gives every single girl the same number, he's just faking you out. That's a pointless rate call, and you shouldn't even try him again. Have another friend try him and maybe he'll do it for real. But you better know there might be a reason he faked the rate call with you, if he kind of recognized your voice and thought he knew it was you and he didn't want to hurt your feelings.

22. Tiny Broken Soldiers

Camille's dad almost never came out of the bedroom at all, which was fine with me, and he never came out with his arm showing. The arm got shot in the war, and the shrapnel made a meal out of him. When Camille described it to me, the shriveled-raisin skin over his flag tattoo, what the arm actually looks like under his clothes, I had a nightmare that night. I had a nightmare the next night too, just from imagining it, and a lot more nights. My mom said maybe I shouldn't play at Camille's house so much, but I didn't listen.

We were running around the neighborhood like usual, but when we came home that afternoon, Mean Mr. Brown-House was coming down Camille's front walk in his slow stiff way. He didn't look at us as we passed each other, and there was her dad in the doorway. He was wearing his gray pants and big black shoes and his undershirt and black suspenders like my grandfather. And there was his arm. I wanted to turn around and run home, but then I'd be there next to Mean Mr. Brown-House, so I stayed with Camille and tried not to look at her dad's horrible arm. In a way, it wasn't as bad as I'd imagined it. It looked like a baby's arm, stuck into a grown man's arm socket, twisted with Indian burns and then left there limp. His face looked so mad it was like it sucked all the angry out of that crooked little arm.

"You've been at it again."

"What did he say?" Camille stood tall even though I felt

like I was shrinking like Alice in Wonderland after she drinks "drink me."

Over our heads, Mr. Broderick watched Mean Mr. Brown-House march off down the road like a robot with rusty joints.

"We weren't at anything," Camille said.

"Get inside." Her dad pushed the door wide with his OK arm. I wondered again if I should run home, but Camille grabbed my hand and yanked me in with her.

"That old liar," she said. "Don't listen to him."

Her dad stopped in the living room and turned to face us. "How dare you?"

My heart banged big and hard.

"Get in here," he said.

I'd almost never been in the Brodericks' living room. Kids don't play in living rooms. The carpet was gray and shiny, and pressed down where a lot of shoes had stood on it. Like the fur on a hard dead rat. He said, "Get your brother's soldiers."

I felt air catch in my throat. Camille's brother Byron is only two years older than us, but he's strong and meaner than any neighbor we've ever bothered. He stutters and I think he gets embarrassed and takes it out on us if we get in his way. I once asked Camille if he was like the lion with a thorn in his paw, and she said no, he's the lion who will claw your head off, and there's no thorn to pull, so don't even try. I wasn't planning on trying.

"But he's not home." Camille suddenly didn't sound so tall. She had another brother once, Oswald, the oldest kid in their family, but he died when she was a baby. Camille's the youngest. There was a picture of Oswald on the mantle in a silver frame. A sniper in Vietnam got him. He was named after his dad. Oswald Broderick Junior. President Nixon pulled the American soldiers out of there, but a whole lot of them came home in boxes before he did. Coming home in a box means you're dead. That's what happened to Oswald Junior. Camille has two other brothers at boarding school, but Byron can't go there for some reason.

"And his marbles." Mr. Broderick didn't yell or anything, but there was no way not to do what he said. He looked at me, like he could read my mind. "And you stay put."

Camille left the room, and her dad stared at me. "You have no idea what you owe that man. We all owe him. He had to come over here, with his knees, and he said, they're at it again, Camille and her friend."

"We didn't do anything." It was obvious even to me, from the sound of my voice, that I was lying. I was seven. And I was scared. I know that's no excuse.

"Stay here." Her dad walked out of the room and left me there alone.

I knew we shouldn't have picked Mean Mr. Brown-House. Camille didn't want to ring his doorbell because of her dad's history, but I said we should. He's younger than her dad, but he seems older. He was a general or something important. He might just seem older though because Camille's dad got one dead arm, but Mean Mr. Brown-House got two bad legs from the war so he has to walk like a creaky old man. I wished we hadn't picked his house.

Shrapnel is a word that sounds exactly like what it is.

I really wanted to go home. I thought I might wet my pants. I think if you can tell that you might, then you probably have enough control of your bladder that you won't. I had on purple corduroy pants, with flares. Not full bell bottoms, which make it hard to run. If a person is very uncomfortable, they should leave and not worry about seeming rude. I know this, but it's different when you're at your friend's house. Camille's dad came back in with something in a plastic bag, and then Camille came in with two navy blue velvet bags, yellow drawstrings all tied up, one in each hand. My brother Chris has toy soldiers too, and he keeps his in the same kind of velvet drawstring bag from a liquor bottle. She stretched the bags toward her dad.

"Dump them out."

"Byron never lets me –"

"Dump them."

She emptied the first bag onto the floor, and I was just a little excited that we were dumping her brother's soldiers out and her dad would have to take the blame. But then he kicked the soldiers on the gray carpet, made them scatter from the couch to the fire place in a path. I watched his hard black shoe kick at Byron's little soldiers, hoping the shoe was softer than it looked. Hoping the soldiers were stronger than they looked.

"Please, Daddy."

"What did that man ever do to you?" Her dad yelled at her, and I held my breath. "What did he ever do to you? Do you know the pain when a man like that has to walk across the floor to answer his door? To have to come over here and tell me? Do you have any idea?"

"No, Sir."

"No, Sir," I repeated.

Her dad untwisted his plastic bag, all with his one good hand, and he poured dry rice onto the bricks near the fireplace. It made no sense. Then he grabbed the second bag from Camille, and he dumped the marbles out among the soldiers lying awkwardly and green every which way, kneeling, standing, prone with rifles, upside down, some with helmets, some without. He held the limp, empty purple-blue bag in his limp, twisted hand.

"We won't do it again," Camille whispered.

"You sure won't. Shoes off." A scattering of BBs glimmered among the soldiers and marbles, little pellets of silver and copper on the gray carpet. Chris and I have never been allowed to have BB guns. People think they're toys, but they can kill you.

"I have to go home," I said.

"And socks."

"My mom said –"

"Go now, and you will not be welcome back here," her dad said. "Ever."

"Ok," I whispered. Camille was kneeling by me, taking off her shoes, and staring at the soldiers and marbles on the carpet. I thought she understood. I started to move toward the door. Her dad held up his hand.

"Go now, and I will call your parents and tell them exactly what went on over here today and why. If you don't want them to know what you did, you stay."

I took a step back and bent over to take off my shoes and socks.

"I thought so," he said. "You don't want to tell your parents. The first smart thing all day. Now get moving, slowly, heel to toe."

"What?" I didn't mean to ask out loud, but I had my answer just by watching Camille. Carefully, we both hobbled forward over the soldiers, their tiny rifles cutting us and snapping under our feet, their hard plastic edges digging into the tender skin between our toes. The soldiers were killing our feet, and I knew Byron would then kill us for real. He'd be furious. Every snap of a soldier breaking hurt more.

"Slowly!" Mr. Broderick yelled. "Think about what that man feels in his feet, his knees. Slowly! That man whose doorbell you like to ring, the pain every time he has to answer his door for two snotty girls."

The human foot has more than 100 muscles and tendons and soft parts. I read it in the encyclopedia. Most of my 100 soft parts found at least one sharp soldier on the carpet. There are 26 bones in a foot, and I think all 26 of mine found a marble. By the time I reached the mantle, to stand on the grains of rice, my feet were on fire. I had tears streaming down my face, but I wasn't crying. I came face-to-face with Oswald Junior. He wasn't smiling in his picture, but even though the picture was black-and-white, it had a light blue

sort of background, and he looked like a nice person. I
hated that sniper who killed him. He was eighteen. I hoped
someone killed that sniper right back, even if he had a nice
Vietnamese family and little brothers and sisters too. Maybe
it's bad to feel that way, wishing someone would get killed.
Maybe I only felt that way because my feet were stinging like
ice and flames in cuts. And because I knew what we did was
bad, but I still didn't think it was fair.

I turned around and Camille's dad wasn't there.

I sniffed hard. "This is better," I whispered. "The rice."

Camille stood stiff. "It's not better."

"Can I go now?"

"It's not done." She bent to look at her naked knees below
the hem of her red skirt. "There's always three. Trinity. He's
coming back."

Her dad came in with the kitchen timer and thrust it at
Camille.

"Three minutes. Why don't you pray while you're
kneeling."

Camille set the timer, put it on the mantle, and knelt on
the rice. I knelt next to her, and the rice and bricks dug into
my knees, even through my corduroys, while Oswald Junior
looked out into the living room over our heads and the timer
clicked and her dad watched us kneel there. I wished I could
somehow give her some fabric from my pants. I felt terrible
for her naked knees and for Mean Mr. Brown-House if this is
how he felt every day just walking in his own house, and for
Oswald Junior who died, and President Nixon who probably
was only ever trying his hardest to do the right thing when
everything got all messed up and everything that started
out messed up just got worse, and I felt terrible for Camille's
parents and Camille's dad's limp baby arm and his wrinkled
tattoo that was probably once really cool for a proud young
soldier-guy with a cigarette in his mouth in a black-and-
white photo with a water-colored background, and a wife

back home worrying about him, and now it's just wrinkled green ink on an old man's weird broken arm, in a room with two girls who are nothing but trouble. But as bad as I felt for him, I wished I could somehow trade Oswalds and put Camille's dad in the picture frame and her nice, handsome dead brother in the room with us instead. My face was wet with tears. Camille's eyes were streaming too. I could tell if we cried out loud though, it would be worse.

"Get up," her dad said. "Clean it all up." He kicked the marbles and soldiers. Tiny dismembered bayonets stuck in the carpet like needles. "Be quick before your brother sees what you've done."

When he let me go, I ran home the whole way, my feet stinging inside my saddle shoes. I told my mom all of it. She wasn't mad about the Ding Dong Ditch 'em, because seven-year- olds do foolish things. She wasn't mad about the punishment Mr. Broderick picked for us, because grown-ups also do foolish things – although she said it was wrong to use Byron's toy soldiers for the punishment since he had nothing to do with it. But she was still really mad about one thing, and she made my dad call Mr. Broderick because they know his type, and it had to come from my dad. No grown-up should ever threaten a child with a secret not to tell their own parents. That's a very slippery slope, Mister!

I didn't go back to Camille's house for a long time, and we never went to Mean Mr. Brown-House's house again, not even to apologize.

23. Something Else about Ex-President Nixon

One thing about President Nixon that's only fair to say, now that we've been through President Ford and now we're on to President Carter is that President Nixon did a lot of good things, and the Watergate scandal doesn't mean his presidency didn't do a lot of good stuff. He's the one who got the soldiers who were still alive out of Vietnam, after all. He might even still be in office if they hadn't changed the rules to make the maximum eight years. If Watergate hadn't happened, who knows how things would be different? You can't think about all the what-might-have-beens though, or it will make you crazy.

Maybe President Nixon didn't even want to go along with the Watergate thing, but his advisors said he'd never win the presidency if they didn't bend the rules a little. People think integrity is an all-or-nothing proposition, but I think it's more like a bead on a string. It slides a little, and you just want to be sure when someone notices, it's in the right place. Everyone does stuff that's not one-hundred-hundred percent perfect all the time. You can still have integrity with just a little bit of sliding. In fact, you probably need to learn to accept yourself and accept the fact that there's always some sliding if you're human.

But our country is founded on the importance of telling the truth. Like how George Washington admitted "I cannot tell a lie, I chopped down the cherry tree." If it was my cherry tree, and I looked forward to making my family a cherry pie every spring, I would be irate if my son chopped it down. Also, what little boy gets ahold of a saw or an axe like that? It must have taken a long time to chop it down, so he would have had to be out there unsupervised a long time. That's really bad! Maybe old George was really great to admit what he did, and maybe he was a great first President of the United States, but there's still a lot about that story I'm not sure I like. Even if I'm not a big fan of cherry pie.

President Nixon is a Quaker though, which means he's opposed to war. I'm sure he was desperate to get those troops home. And I like how he tried to become friends with China, which is important for our two countries. Although my dad says we better watch out or Chinese goods and warehouse clubs are going to ruin the American economy. Those people can crank out top quality merchandise for next to nothing, and no matter how many times you tell an American to "buy American," they won't bat an eye if the price is cheaper elsewhere. And they'll drive miles to buy in bulk. He says we should watch out for that attitude too. We shouldn't entertain ourselves by buying and storing a bunch of things we don't need. And we shouldn't buy stuff without commitment and just return it. Things are getting out of hand. Things and people and people's compulsions and theories of entitlement. People should work hard and show some respect! My mom says, "OK, Al, enough from the soapbox."

24. Return on Investment

O ne more business thing to understand Return on Investment. Let's say you invite ten girls to your birthday party and all of them are nice and bring good presents but you decide to invite one girl who's new and pretty shy, but you heard that at her old school they give *really* good presents. You might want to invite her as your tenth friend to see if it's true, and maybe you will get a great present. You should invite her just to be nice, of course, but right now I'm talking about the investment.

Last year I invited Barbie Malone, and even though she couldn't come to my party, and so she didn't give me a present, it was like an ice-breaker and now we're friends. Our families are going to the Nelson Gallery for a picnic on the lawn together in the spring because it turns out her mom grew up in Boston, so she has some things in common with my mom, because they're both from big cities with public transportation.

Aunt Lula and Uncle Frank gave me an instamatic camera, which is one of my best presents ever. I know deep down their present didn't have anything to do with my inviting Barbie Malone to my party, but some people think everything's connected. Maybe it was a good deed that I invited Barbie. Well, some people also say "no good deed goes unpunished," but that's just a bad attitude speaking.

And everybody else is friends with Barbie now too. Lizzie, Annie, Page, Camille, Constance, Shelly, everyone. My mom talks about the ripple effect, like you throw a pebble in the lake and it makes a ripple that spreads out and out, especially if the lake is calm. That's how good deeds and nice people work. It seems like magic, but it's just nature.

25. Lemonade Stand

Running a business doesn't just come naturally to everybody, but it's actually not that hard to figure out. If you know how to do a lemonade stand, you'll know basically everything. Like first of all, if it's a lemonade stand, just sell lemonade. If you try to sell perfume at your lemonade stand, no one will buy any, so it's a waste of time mixing all those little bottles, and a waste of space on your table. I learned this the hard way. That's a good tip for life. If someone tells you they learned something the hard way, you should try to remember what they learned.

Second of all, try to get your inventory for free. Inventory is the thing you're selling. So if your mom will make your lemonade for you, it will be free. Also, if she makes it, it will taste good, which is quality control. And whoever makes it, that's your labor. So your mom is your labor pool which is your group of workers. I don't know why they call it a pool. In the olden days the secretaries were called the secretarial pool, like in the ad agencies in New York, maybe because they would go swimming together on weekends. With a lemonade stand, if your workers are your brother and two of his friends, they will probably get bored and leave before a car comes to buy lemonade, so you might have to promise to give your brother your chocolate pudding after dinner to keep him working for you. That's not a bribe, which is a bad thing – it's just being a good boss.

Every time you sell a cup of lemonade, ask the person who

bought it to please tell their friends. That's marketing. Also your sign is marketing. (Make it BIG). And if you put a sign on Ward Parkway, that's marketing too, but I think it could also be advertising. I'm not too sure about the difference. I think advertising is something you pay for, so like, if they made you pay a dollar to someone on Ward Parkway to hang your sign there, maybe that's advertising. You have to decide if enough people will come from Ward Parkway to your house or not, and if a lot will come, then it's worth paying for your ad. That's your investment. You should never make any investment unless the money you will make from it will probably turn out to be more than the investment.

You really should try to hire people who do their job because they love it so much the money doesn't matter, but unfortunately for your business, they also have to get paid. But that's OK, if you pay a lot and give good feedback, like tell them when they're doing a good job, or how they can do a better job, then they will like working for you. And they will tell their friends to work for you too. That's good because someone always has to go home or they get bored before you're done.

I forgot to mention you also have to have cups and lemons and sugar and everything. All the stuff you have to buy and your labor and your poster board and everything you have to pay for is your overhead, like the roof over your head. Even if you get some of it for free, you should write down what it would have cost so you know what your business really is doing. That's really important! Keep track of everything.

One last thing, don't charge too much, but don't give it away too cheap! People know "you get what you pay for," and if it's good lemonade, they will expect to pay a good, fair price.

One more thing about money. Write down everything you make in black, and if anything costs you money, write it in red. You can remember red is negative because they both have an "e" in the front. After you do all your math at the end of the day, if your number is black, that means you made money, you made a profit, and you can tell people, "We're in the black." That's easy to remember because black is beautiful.

Also that's why it's bad luck to sign a check in red, because it might make you go broke. Maybe that's just a superstition, but why risk it? Even my dad says so, and he's always very practical. He carries a black pen, just in case.

26. Sandwiches

My mom's relatives had another good saying about water, not about the ripple effect, but about the ocean. "If you throw bread out on the water, it comes back sandwiches." I think it's from the Bible, but they might have changed it because they're not Bible people. Sometimes I wish they were, or we were, so I would know all those sayings. She says I can read it myself if I want to know them, and I think I will. But I have the impression my parents might be mad if I do, because don't normal parents make their children go to church or synagogue or temple or whatever, and in normal families, the children don't want to go? So if I read the Bible on my own because I want to, it's like we're in an upside down house.

Also I'm not sure they would talk about sandwiches in the Bible. I think they probably only ate slaughtered animals back then, and fish and plants.

27. Public Speaking

I have a tip about public speaking. This isn't a "secret" to overcoming a fear of it. I think it's cheating to tell someone you have a secret when it's not a secret. This is just a tip.

And not everyone's afraid of public speaking, but if you are, you just have to know how to tell yourself something so it's convincing. Some people will say to picture your audience in their underwear, so you'd be looking at your audience like they're all fools who forgot to get dressed, so you won't be intimidated. But who wants to make a speech for a bunch of fools? Instead, just tell yourself it's a really nice audience and they want to hear what you have to say. You can tell yourself that because it's true! A few might be jerks who want you to trip going up on stage, or mess up with the microphone, or stutter, or forget your lines, but mostly, they want you to be successful. And these are important people who like you! They're not idiots in their underwear – they're extremely well-dressed, in fact. Like scarves with fancy knots and skirts and suits, and they love you and whatever you're talking about.

Also, it helps it to squeeze your knees at the podium. No one needs to know you're doing it. We have to do a lot of speeches at school. It's good practice in case someday you might be in politics or a teacher. The thing with the knees really works. So maybe that part is a good secret, after all.

28. Racing for the Mailbox

Paul Mayer was the fastest boy in first grade at my old school. If you take Wornall Road, his house is on the way to mine. He runs like lightning, like a flash of lightning. He runs like he's invisible and you only knew he was there by the rush of air he left behind him, when the leaves in the bushes flutter, and one thousand yellow butterflies all lift up into the sky like they're celebrating how fast he is. Also, you can smell the air, like how it smells when it's about to rain, because of how the air moves when he races past, invisible. And every time, there is nothing until the end, except that dark brown wet smell of dirt or earth or leaves or whatever, and all those butterflies, and then Paul Mayer is there panting at the finish line like it was no big deal. He doesn't even have to bend over to breathe.

Every time we did races at school, even with other classes with older boys, he always won. People will probably write books about him, history books about his greatness, and they will read them in every school in the whole world, because he's so fast, like a super-human person in a myth. Paul Mayer!

One time, I walked home the way he went, and I saw him on the street on Wornall Road. No one else was there, and I asked him to race me, and he said OK. End of the road to the mailbox. On your mark, get set, go. We were neck-and-neck until the end, but I touched the mailbox first. Our hands both went to it but it was my hand that slammed the blue metal mailbox first. Like ba-BOOM. Not, you know, way ahead, boom-boom. Almost the same time, just not quite. It's like my whole body was pounding when I saw my hand land there. Not just my heart, but my legs and arms and lungs and everything. Even the tips of my fingers that slammed the blue mailbox. Maybe he let me win, I don't know. But we said we'd never tell, and I almost never did because no one would ever believe I could beat Paul Mayer in a race, and actually, no one believed he would even race me.

And also – I don't think I believed I could do it again, if someone ever made us do it again for a re-play. If I could beat him in front of people, it would embarrass him since I'm a girl, and I wouldn't want to do that anyway. It was just my lucky day that one day – racing for the mailbox – and a little secret I could keep for me. That's the best thing to do with a secret.

29. Red Sneakers

I might be the second fastest girl in our class but I always get butterflies when I'm up at kickball. My mom says everyone gets butterflies. No one wants to let down their team. Being on show is a difficult thing, like public speaking which is normally people's worst fear. Mike Harper is the fastest boy at this school, maybe even faster than Paul Mayer at my old school. Everyone picks him first. He's black. In my family, we used to say "dark-skinned people" when we moved here, but everyone always asked what does that mean, do you mean black? So I realized if I'm going to live here, I better say "black" like everyone else, even though black people are mostly brown, so it isn't even accurate. I should probably ask Mike Harper what he wants to be called. He's the one who ought to get to choose dark-skinned or black or colored or negro or whatever he wants. I don't mind being called white, even though obviously, that's totally wrong too. I'm more like light peach. If you go by the crayon colors, peach is as close as you get. It's a shame though, because nobody's peach and all the drawings look ridiculous, like the person has a disease. If you're dark-skinned, the brown crayon isn't right either. If you're Mexican or Cuban or Puerto Rican, you could be all different shades of brown to tan to lighter than me. The bottom line is no matter who you are and where your ancestors come from, there's never the right crayon for you. You're probably in between the peach and the brown. You can melt crayons in the sun, but they don't blend the way you'd hope, and it doesn't work to make new colors.

Lizzie is the fastest girl. They pick her first, and sometimes they pick me next. My shoes are the rounded-toe kind, and they're red. In my family we call them sneakers instead of tennis shoes. I wear them a size too small because my mom says that makes you fast. She learned that at summer camp. She was the fastest girl in her class and her camp. They used to call her Tommy because she was a tom boy. I'm not a tom boy, but I do sometimes like boy things. But I like girl things too though, like lip gloss.

Lip gloss is only appropriate for a short period of your life when you're growing up, but you're not quite there yet. You should use Chapstick until you are ten. When you hit double digits you'll probably get a lip gloss for your birthday, and then you can have lip gloss as long as you want, but pretty soon you will probably want to switch to real lipstick – like in high school. So you should enjoy lip gloss while you can, for two or three years. When you first wear lipstick someone will probably make fun of you, and you'll have to decide how to deal with that. I recommend saying "yeah, so what?" but I admit, that's not what I did.

Last year I wore lipstick one day, just to try it out, and Constance accused me of wearing it, and I lied and said I wasn't, so she made me press my lips onto a piece of paper to prove it, and I hardly pressed at all, so nothing showed, but it was bad to lie about it. It made me feel bad, I mean, and I think it made some people not like Constance for how she was treating me, and it made some people not like me, or not trust me. Everyone assumes Constance is really nice because she looks so innocent, with big dark brown eyes, almost black, that she blinks a lot, and her hair is like wispy silk, light brown that turns blond in summer, and it flies around and never stays in her ponytail. Her mom was a model in Paris for two seasons, and she has those same kind of brown-black eyes and they called her La Mouse because she must have been soft and furry and tiny looking, even though she's very tall. They have magazine pictures of her in a swimsuit and false eyelashes framed in their living room. Her pelvic bones stick out in all her pictures, and her collarbones. I think Constance is also proud of her collarbones. My mom says some men find "waifishness" attractive, and that's what a tall skinny mouse is, a "waif." They look like they need someone strong to take care of them, and certain men worry about those ladies and hope they are the strong man who can be the hero. Mom says Constance will always get attention because she's so pretty, and she's lucky to also be so smart in case she attracts the wrong kind of attention. She also says plenty of men prefer women who are strong and street smart, and every single person can be pretty to someone. She says there's someone out there for everyone.

But my advice is don't rush to wear lipstick. Next year I probably will wear it every day because I'll be 13, and by then in some states, girls can already get married. Elvis Presley's wife was 14, I think. Maybe that was just the olden days though. My mom got married at 25, and that seems like a reasonable age. By the time I'm older, maybe 30 would be a more reasonable age. Whatever you do, don't get married unless you're ready and you're sure it's the right husband, because the rest of your life might last a really long time.

But you should try to enjoy your lip gloss time while you can. Some people like Bubble Gum Kissing Potion, but I think roll-on lip gloss is too sticky. Your hair gets in it. Lip Smackers Root Beer is my favorite. Lizzie gave me Lip Smackers 7-Up for my birthday, and it's good too. Constance gave me Love's Baby Soft perfume that smells really nice. The bottle is pink and baby blue. I told my mom I'm going to wear Love's Baby Soft forever, but she said she doubts it because a person's tastes change as you develop, and it's really just for girls. She wears Charlie and Enjoli and Jean Nate, that all have catchy songs on TV. "I can bring home the bacon, fry it up in a pan, and never, never let you forget you're a man. Enjoli." It might be true about my tastes about perfume changing, but I promise I will always love dogs and ice skating and hockey and swimming and Judy Blume, even when I'm grown up.

I hate that word "develop." It seems like the human body is doing something totally out of control, growing big blobs on itself where they don't need to be. Every science class is always about girls developing. Rounded hips, uterus, ovaries, fallopian tubes, blood flow, cervix, eggs. Blah blah blah. Wash your hair, sit up straight, shave your legs, cross your legs, cross your heart 18-hour Playtex Bra. Even worse is when my mom talks about "heavy petting" and "experimenting." I seriously want to barf. In fourth grade, we had to watch a movie about sexual intercourse in the multipurpose room, and they didn't even separate the boys from the girls for the show. I was sitting next to John, and I thought I might actually die.

My second favorite Lip Smacker is Watermelon. Mrs. Campbell said girls are getting sick because Bonne Bell uses castor oil in Lip Smackers, and we lick it off and swallow it all day, especially the girls who wear their Lip Smackers on a cord necklace. But I think she just finds it annoying in class. I don't lick it off. What would the point be in that? If you're only wearing lip gloss for a short time in your life, you better train yourself not to lick it off. Can you imagine a grown woman licking off her red lipstick? Ridiculous! You always have to do stuff with an eye on the future.

But I want to say something about my red sneakers and roller skates. The sneakers fit inside metal roller skates, although I don't like skates with metal wheels like that. Skating on the sidewalk makes my teeth rattle, and sometimes, tree roots push up the edges of the sidewalk and trip you, and sometimes there are pebbles to make you fall. Also, I can never turn the skate key tight enough, so a skate always comes loose under my foot, with the red leather strap still around my ankle. And if my dad turns the skate key, it always goes too tight so you can't get it open to give the skates to your brother. I guess that's not about my sneakers as much as it's about the roller skates. Chris likes skateboarding more than roller skating anyway, and he almost never falls. He's very coordinated and athletic, he just doesn't have a killer instinct for team sports. That's what my dad says. I guess if he is someday in the Olympics, it will be an individual sport where you don't have to be a killer. Too bad they don't have skateboarding in the Olympics. My dad doesn't have a killer instinct either, although he has a lot of amazing talents and a head for business. A killer instinct seems like a bad thing to have, unless of course you're a killer for a living, like a hitman. And that would come with all kinds of other problems.

Lizzie had a roller disco birthday party when she turned 11, with rental skates with rubber wheels. I don't like the roller rink because you can tell the teenagers wish you weren't there. When they play a slow song and it's dark with colored lights and the mirrored ball, and the stinky smoke machine, the teenagers skate around with their arms around each other and sometimes a girl will even stick her hand in her boyfriend's back pocket or vice versa. They usually have a big comb in their other back pocket. It seems really awkward. I can't imagine ever wanting to stick my hand in some boy's pocket. Maybe when I'm a teenager I'll suddenly be a different person with different ideas about skates and lipstick and hands in pockets.

30. Facedown

A lready last week, there were two presents under our Christmas tree, shiny red boxes, because our mom likes to get a jump on Christmas. Mine has a green plaid bow in gros-grain ribbon like you'd sew on your clothes, and Chris' has a gold bow. Mom makes bows with lots of loops because wrapping presents is an art. She also can do Jacob's Ladder with a Chinese jump rope, so I think she likes ribbons and strings in general. We always keep the bows when we throw the wrapping paper in the fire. This year, I want to keep that plaid ribbon in my room. We're not supposed to touch the presents under the tree, but sometimes we still do. I don't shake my presents because something could get broken.

Most families don't have the tree up yet, but we always put ours up on Thanksgiving, while the football game's on TV and the dishes are in the middle of getting done, and there's a new plate of white-meat turkey in the fridge that I don't like as much as dark unless you add mayonnaise on your sandwich. My mom makes scrambled eggs with the leftovers the next day, but no one really wants to eat them. She's the only mom I know who does that. Dad puts the lights on the tree, and then Mom and Chris and I do the rest so Dad doesn't miss the game. It's a fake green tree this year with a red velvet tree skirt with satin tassels that feel good to rub between your fingers. We are not a family that believes in tinsel because it makes a mess. Camille's family always had a ton of tinsel. I never go there any more.

The shiny red present for me looks like a shoebox, and the one for Chris is a bigger box that might be a Lite-brite. That's what he wants. I read his letter to Santa before we mailed it. We still mail Santa letters every year even though we both know about Santa. At least I think Chris knows. He's 10 years old, and most kids know by the time they're 10, but I don't want to mention it in case he doesn't know. Pretending not to know isn't so dumb.

Some years I don't even know what I want till I write my letter. Time sometimes slips by and you forget to even think about what you want. If you don't know what you want, you probably won't get it, or if you do, you probably won't appreciate it that much. My present probably isn't shoes, it's probably a re-used shoe box holding something else. I asked for a 45-record for our antique jukebox of "Le Freak." It's by Chic. "Ah... freak out!" A 45-record can fit in a shoe box.

Chris and I were by the tree, lying on the tree skirt. Once it's all loaded with presents, there wouldn't be room to lie down there. I was rubbing my palm on the velvet, and Chris shook his box. There was no noise. A Lite-brite comes with a million little plastic pegs, and even packed in baggies, they'd probably rattle. I didn't say anything, but I knew what he was thinking by the way his face crinkled up. Maybe I should have said it could still be a Lite-brite.

Chris pushed the present back under the tree, far under there, where the pine needles are prickery on your face, and he lay facedown on the tree skirt like he was dead and didn't move. His hands were up near his face.

I poked him in the side to make him laugh. When he wears his plain white cotton turtleneck, for some reason I always want to poke him in the side.

"Don't." His voice sounded strangled.

I poked him again. Sometimes it takes doing a thing twice to make someone laugh.

He shoved his arms down by his sides so I couldn't get him, but I wedged my finger in there anyway and poked him again. He didn't move, so I jabbed his butt, the pocket of his brown corduroys, and he squirmed around and then went straight back facedown on the red velvet.

"Leave me alone." Now his voice was more than strangled. It was all tight, and I could tell he was crying. We didn't even know it wasn't a Lite-brite.

"What's wrong with you?" I lay down next to him with my face near his under the branches where I normally wouldn't want to put my face. I didn't touch him. Our mom was upstairs. I could hear her sewing machine, the clicking noise when she grabs the metal lever to lift the needle from a seam she's just done. I like the sound of the thread when she finishes a seam and goes back and forth over the final half-inch or so, and then that clicking. I wondered if Chris didn't snap out of it, if she would come down on her own or if I'd have to get her.

He put his hands up on his head and started pushing his face into the velvet, pushing his fingers into his hair, pushing, and crying. I grabbed his wrist and tried to pull his hand off his head, but he suddenly shoved his whole body out from under the tree and ran to the kitchen with me struggling to run behind him, and he went right out the back door without his coat or anything. The screen door slammed but he didn't even shut the main door. He left it wide open. He'd only just gone out, but I didn't see him outside.

"Mom!" I yelled up the stairs.

She and Barley came running down. She grabbed Chris' coat and got Barley on his leash and went out to find my brother. I have enough money saved up I could get him a Lite-brite myself, but somehow I knew that wasn't what it was about, even though I had no idea what it was about.

I waited for them to come back. I sat in the kitchen with my elbows on the table and my chin in my hands. I closed my eyes and counted. I tried breathing so shallowly that my body wouldn't move at all. It was starting to get dark, and I still waited. I didn't turn on the TV or call anyone on the phone. I sat in the kitchen listening to the clock ticking. I didn't turn on the light because it wasn't dark enough yet. If you ever lose someone, you should stay put so when they come to their senses and come back, you'll be there and not out looking for them. It's different if you're stuck on the subway in New York and your mom gets out of the train car. If that happens you should get out at the next stop, but be sure your whole family knows that rule, so she'll get back on the next train and she knows to get out at the next stop to find you.

It was starting to get pretty dark. I pretended I was one of the Von Trapp family singers when they're hiding in that church yard, behind that big gravestone or monument and the Nazis are coming with their flashlights, and they have to be dead still and silent. I pretended I was Liesl and when she sees Rolf and cries out, I pretended I could change the story, even though *The Sound of Music* is non-fiction. I would be Liesl who stays quiet like she's supposed to so they don't get caught.

I heard a car door slam and then the back door creaked open and Dad came in the kitchen. He turned the light on and saw me there.

"She found him near Brookside," he said. "She called from the payphone."

I nodded at my dad. I wanted to ask if everything was OK, or where she found him, but it felt like I might cry if I talked.

"What upset him?" Dad put a brown McDonald's bag down on the table.

"Nothing. I didn't do anything."

Dad pulled out a hamburger and told me to eat it before it got cold. It was already cold. The pickle and little onion squares had seeped juices into the bread. I wasn't hungry anyway. Dad had a Quarter Pounder, and he ate the whole thing in three bites, like he was offended by it and had to get rid of it fast. He sat by me not saying anything, and I could hear him breathing through his nose and chewing his hamburger and still the clock ticking. I wanted to say something funny so he'd start talking, but nothing was funny at all. I heard his throat swallowing.

Finally Mom and Chris came in the house, and Barley ran to me. His fur was cold and soft under my hand. My face felt very tight and I almost started crying which makes no sense, but I was really happy they were home. I gave Barley a French fry.

Chris took off his coat and sat down at the table. His white turtleneck had mud on the front and the arms. I couldn't picture how it got there, or where he'd been. Dad pushed a hamburger in its paper wrapping at him. We didn't have plates on the table – just napkins from McDonald's. Not even any drinks. Mom stood by the sink and pulled open a cellophane bag of Barley's dog food and dumped it in his bowl. I think he was the only one who was hungry. We all listened to the metal of his dog tags clink against his bowl as he chomped his dinner.

"Do you want to tell your father what upset you?" Mom came and sat down next to Chris. I thought they might make me leave the room if it was something personal, but they didn't. There were grass stains on his white shirt too. He still seemed cold to me, like he'd brought the outside in with him, and he smelled like grass.

He pulled off a piece of his bun with his fingers but he dropped it on the paper and rubbed his thumb against his fingers to knock off the sesame seeds.

Mom stood back up, went to the counter, and then came back to the table. She put a copy of *Time Magazine* on the table. "The Cult of Death" it said on the front. I knew what the story was because everyone was talking about it at school. A bunch of people drank poison Kool-Aid because they had a crazy leader who made them do it, and they committed suicide instead of running away. Almost a thousand people. His name was Jim Jones and they were so brainwashed they named their commune Jonestown. If they tried to run away, someone shot them.

"I picked up this copy in the grocery story, so we could talk about it. He saw it at school."

I hadn't seen the magazine and I wanted to look, but I was a little afraid. In my mind, I tried to be Liesl Von Trapp again, staying still and quiet.

"This?" Dad put his hand gently on the magazine. "These people were insane. This whole thing was insane."

"They were families," my mom said. "Children. Mothers gave that poison to their children. You can understand –"

"Crazies. Religious freaks turned communists. They were brainwashed." He turned to my brother. "Chris, this has nothing to do with you or us or anyone we know."

My brother breathed in hard and short, only in-breaths, that stair-step way like when you're only going up-up-up. He said, "I know."

I felt close to crying too, like my breathing was on that same staircase with my brother. I tried to concentrate on the cold French fries and the napkin in front of me. They looked like fake food. Yellow sticks that would make you very sick if you ate one. I was sorry I'd given one to Barley.

My mom slid the magazine toward herself and opened it. She flipped several pages, the noise of the slick paper as she did it going wisp, wisp, wisp. She stopped. "This," she said.

The kitchen light reflected a glowing white circle in the magazine paper, but I could still see the picture. There was a family lying facedown on the ground. They wore jeans. Tight jeans, one in a sweater, one in an orange t-shirt. You could see their arms and their hair, and right in the middle, a little boy or girl, probably boy, with little brown legs, and a little blue romper, snapped closed under his bottom, and you could see his diaper at the edge, the puffy white diaper peeking out, and his shoes, the white rubber soles of his sneakers, with the same pattern in the treads as my sneakers and Chris'. His mom's arm was around him, and they were all facedown in the dirt. All the pictures showed all those people at Jonestown, facedown like that, dead. I wanted to be there, to pick up that baby and hold him in his little blue romper with the snaps and that diaper on my arm, go back in time just a couple of weeks and go to that place, that island where the crazy Jonestown people were, and prop him up on my hip, take him away, and protect him. Maybe that's what Chris was thinking too. But no one can go back in time, and considering his own mother gave that baby the poison, it's not like I could have done anything if I'd been there, and neither could Chris. If we'd been there, we'd have ended up face-down just like as the rest of them. I felt bad, though, that the whole thing upset Chris the way it did, but not me. Maybe it should have upset me. I agreed with my dad. Those people had nothing to do with us. Chris is a nicer person than I am.

"He was on drugs," my mom said. "For weeks. He was very ill and sleep deprived, they're saying, and he went crazy."

"He started out crazy. Religious freaks. What's shocking is the followers. All their money, their lives, their children's lives. Religion." My dad pushed the magazine away hard, and it fell to the floor, flipped itself over, closed. No one touched it. No one touched the food still on the table. Barley came and sniffed the magazine and walked away uninterested.

"Insanity," my mom said quietly.

"They're sheep. They were idiots. This proves it." My dad pointed at the floor.

My mom put her hand on my brother's shoulder. "Chris, honey, you understand this is a terrible thing that happened, and we'd rather you wouldn't have had to see these pictures at school –"

My dad interrupted. "Every generation has to improve a little on the ignorance of the past, that's our only obligation. The progress we encourage in our children. Generation after generation, forward movement, a little new intelligence." His fists were clenched. "Think it's a coincidence they used Kool-Aid to poison those people? They were all children, even the adults, the way they blindly followed that man. There was to be no improvement there. But this nightmare set these people way back. Their blood lines."

"Well, it stopped them," I said. "Since they're all dead now. It's not like now their kids are going to…"

Chris stared at me, and I stopped talking.

My mom continued rubbing my brother's shoulder. "You must never shy away from understanding terrible things like this, things people do… are capable of doing. If you understand, you can be one of the people who helps make things better."

Chris nodded.

"Our parents would never be like those parents," I said. "They'd never get brainwashed."

Chris glanced at me but didn't say anything. He pulled the sleeves of his shirt down over his hands and kept his fingers tucked in there. It seemed pretty obvious that one of my parents should say to Chris something like *that's right, kiddo, we'd never do anything to hurt you.* But neither of them said a word to agree with me. No kid should have to be afraid of their own mom or dad.

My dad finally stood up. "You remember Patty Hearst? We talked about brainwashing. We also talked about what a free society is, how Americans get to have free will and choice." My dad's voice got louder and both his fists were even tighter.

"He's ten," my mom said. "For goodness sake."

Dad sat back down.

Chris said, "It wasn't their fault they had stupid parents."

The magazine stayed on the floor, and I stared at the table waiting for one of my parents to answer my brother. We aren't supposed to use the word stupid, even though everybody at school says it, including Chris and me.

"Do you think it hurt?" he asked. "When they died?"

"Stomach cramp." My dad shook his head. "It was very fast."

The cold French fries smelled greasy. I wanted to go upstairs and lie down and not think about all those dead people in Jonestown anymore. Patty Hearst supposedly fell in love with her kidnapper and turned into a bank robber with a machine gun. That's not brainwashing, that's flat-out bonkers. They put it on the scoreboard at the Scouts game, when her verdict came out guilty. The crowd all gasped. It's a weird thing to hear a few thousand people gasp at the same time. Some people also said "oh!" and there was all kinds of muttering and they clapped. Mom said everyone had thought she'd get off because her family's rich. That was a weird hockey game. Even the score was weird, since we usually lost, and in the end, it was a tie game, two to two. I didn't even really care about Patty Hearst before they put the news on the scoreboard, but suddenly being there with everyone learning her verdict kind of made me interested. Trouble is I think she was guilty, but I still don't know if it was her fault that she turned bad. I'd probably make an awful juror. A person should know what they believe and stick to it. Anyway, my dad says President Carter is probably going to let her out of jail now because he's a Democrat. "Exonerated" means innocent, as in *Patty Hearst was not exonerated, and the Scouts fans clapped.*

My dad leaned over and picked up the "Cult of Death" magazine. He walked over to the trash under the sink and threw it away. He came back and patted Chris on the head like he was Barley. Somehow that made me feel a lot better.

They kept Chris home from school the rest of this week,

and now there's only one week left before Christmas break. I
don't know if he's going to school this week or not. He has to
talk to a special doctor about his feelings. Normally if a kid
who's not sick gets to miss school for a week, you'd think he's
lucky, or you'd think something was wrong, but that's what
you'd expect in a normal family. And obviously, we're not like
that. At school I'm just saying he has the flu. A little white lie.

31. It's Happening Now

Four years ago, Easter, I was nine, and I invented something kind of useful. The thing is, you can't go back and change the past, even though people can change their minds about earlier decisions. If President Carter lets Patty Hearst out of jail, hopefully she learned her lesson. This is from when Chris and I first started going in to work on Saturdays and I got to use the electric typewriter. It happened in third grade but I wrote about it in fourth. If you don't write everything down, it's tough to keep track!

I was dressed up for Easter and I was outside with Barley, going up the back deck steps. Mom had yelled out the back door twice that I had to come in for indoor pictures. We do some indoors so the wind won't mess up my hair and stuff. And then we take most of our Easter pictures outside, even if it's actually too cold. But it was kind of a nice day, and I wanted to stay outside with Barley. Anyway, I knew Chris probably wasn't ready. People think it only takes one minute for boys to get dressed, or men, but tying a tie is pretty hard, and it actually takes them a long time. I think because they normally don't care so much about what they look like, so on Easter or for a party or their wedding or something, it's probably kind of intimidating to get ready. Anyway, she had yelled twice, but I thought I should still have time.

But after a while, I was on my way to going inside. For some reason I just thought, in two seconds I'm going to be on the top step, and then on the deck – not on the steps anymore. And then I'll be through the back door in the kitchen. But right *now* here I am on the steps. I'm wearing my Easter dress and saddle shoes, and Barley's here with his own fur coat, and it's a little too cold to be outside without a coat for me, but here I am. I have brown hair, and it's clean and brushed because it's Easter, and I know what color brown hair looks like to me, even if maybe it looks different to other people. Maybe my version of brown looks like blond to someone else. How would anyone ever know? But I know what I think I look like, and here I am today, looking like this, just as I am. Here I am – me.

I looked down at the step and I thought, there's my foot, there's my black-and-white saddle shoe. My shoe is kind of scuffed on the toe. Maybe it needs white shoe polish on the white part, especially since it's Easter, and your shoes should look nice. The shoe polish bottle is the squeezy kind, with a sponge tip, which is pretty easy to use, even if you're a child. But my saddle shoes are just the right amount of old. You never want to get caught wearing saddle shoes when it snows because they're so slippery, even after the soles are scuffed. I was thinking all that about my shoes and snow and my hair being brown, and how much more I like the outside pictures than the inside ones, and I was wishing my parents would just come outside with the camera to take our Easter pictures with Barley and my brother dressed up in his dark gray suit with the birds singing and leaves just starting to come out green on the trees… and then suddenly I was just thinking here I am on these steps, and *this* is me, in my own little piece of the world, and this is what's happening *right now*.

I repeated the whole phrase in my head. *This is happening now.* Then later, when it's over I hoped I could think *that was happening "then,"* and it won't be "*now*" anymore, but I bet in my mind I can keep it. The *now*. The steps. My shoe right there, stepping on the middle step. My dress is yellow and my tights are white and scratchy. They're wool. It's chilly and there's some wind making it colder, making the black branches in the tree wave, and the ground is still hard, even though there's no snow anymore. Here's Barley bounding up the steps by my side and panting. He loves the cold. He loves every kind of weather.

The back deck steps are redwood. When they look worn out, we paint them with redwood stain, or sometimes rust-colored paint. Rust seems like a bad color – if there is rust on your car you have to get rid of it because one spot of rust leads to more. The floor can rust out of a car, because the floor's made of metal, and then, if you're sitting on the floor and not on your seat, you could fall through onto the road and die. That happened to a girl in Arkansas. I saw it in the newspaper. Or maybe Alabama. If I was from Alabama, I'd say it all the time: "I am! I am from Alabama!"

But when our deck needs to look new again, they paint it rust. I wish they would call it brownish-red or reddish-brown, but my mom doesn't like words with "ish." She has no respect for anything wishy-washy. She says you should find the right word. The crayon color that matches it is called "bittersweet." I don't mind that color, but I can't stand its name. It makes me think of blood and earwax. I don't even like the pinkish paper label on that crayon. I respect my mom's opinion, but personally, I have no problem with "ish." That paper label really is pinkish. Sometimes the right word is the ish-word! Although I guess you could call it blush or rose or rose-beige. I wonder if using a hyphen like that is also wishy-washy. My mom can be hard to please.

But the point is, I was thinking I bet I can go back in my mind to my black-and-white saddle shoe on the redwood step right here, just by remembering back to thinking *this is happening now*. And now as I'm writing this, Easter is over, it's already the future, and it works. Every time I try it, I can still picture my shoe on the step, and I can still feel that yellow dress on my body and the tights and the cold and the black trees waving with their little green leaf-buds, and it works every time. So if you plan ahead, you can keep a thing from the past and bring it with you into your future, if you want to, and on and on and on.

32. Things That Are Good to Know

1. Never swim without a buddy. Make sure your buddy knows she is your buddy and vice versa.

2. Never point a gun at anyone, including yourself, even if you think it's not loaded.

3. Never get in an elevator if someone who looks suspicious is already in it. If you're already in the elevator and someone suspicious gets in, get out. Don't worry about seeming rude! It's better to be rude than dead.

4. Never pet a dog you don't know. Useful tip: if its tail is wagging, it is probably fine though. (But it's always good to know these rules so then you can decide when to break them).

5. Snakes are not good pets. Having a snake for a pet is unnatural.

6. Never make jokes about other people's races, including Polack jokes, because Polacks are just people from Poland. Also, don't laugh if your friends make these jokes because that will just encourage them.

7. Never clean your gun in the middle of the night.

8. Never say you don't like your dinner if your friend's

mom made it. You can just not eat it. Say "thank you for having me over," but don't say "thank you for the nice dinner," because then you'd be fake.

9. Never buy red paper napkins for a dinner party because if someone spills their drink on their white shirt, and they use a red napkin to wipe it, it will turn the shirt red. It happened to my Aunt Lula when Uncle Frank spilled and he was spitting mad about those napkins and his white shirt. That's what Aunt Lula said. Spitting mad.

10. Also, Aunt Lula said she failed her first driver's test because she didn't look over her shoulder to check for traffic, and you can't trust the rear-view mirror alone. She's a good driver though. She drives the Winnebago when they take it to the beach, so Uncle Frank can sleep in the back. He gets tired because he's a lawyer which means a lot of reading, so he sleeps whenever he can. Aunt Lula wants to get her pilot's license too. She likes big vehicles. She smokes her cigarette and blows the smoke up and laughs and says, "I have an affinity for big vehicles." Aunt Lula's collarbones stick out and she touches them. My mom said no one from New York likes to drive because there's never any parking.

11. If you're afraid to do something, like ride Camel, for instance, because he's a mean horse who puts his ears back and canters when he's supposed to trot, and he trots hard when he's supposed to walk, it's OK to say you don't want to ride him. And then just say it's because you're afraid. Sometimes a grown-up will think they can tease you into doing something by making fun of you for being afraid and keeping it to yourself. So don't keep it to yourself. Just admit it out loud in front of everyone, "Yes, of course I'm afraid

of that crazy horse. I'm not getting up there. He'll run off to Tonganoxie with me and you'll never see me again!" Important note: it's good to exaggerate the result of the bad thing that will happen. Also, for some reason everyone always laughs when you mention Tonganoxie.

12. Stick to your guns! You have to be serious about not doing the thing, whatever it is. If they are still trying to make you ride Camel, say you know someone must have better horsemanship skills than you do, and they should be on Camel. Usually you'll get lucky and a show-off boy will step up to ride him.

13. Don't eat any berries you find outside unless you know what they are. Also, it's best to bring them in and wash them. And don't eat snow very often because it has acid rain that might make you sick. But you can make snow ice cream once or twice every winter. Just add vanilla and sugar. It doesn't actually taste very good.

14. If you are sledding at Suicide Hill and you're going too fast to steer, you have to yell so kids can get out of the way. Or at least you can tell them afterwards that you tried to warn them.

15. Don't put your boots too close to the fire at Suicide Hill, especially if your feet are in them!

33. Forklifts and Pallet Jacks

Aunt Lula has her affinity for big vehicles, and maybe I do too. I got to drive the forklift last weekend with Mr. Darrel. It didn't have a pallet on it, so it was just an empty forklift. Chris and I both move pallets of boxes with the pallet jack – it's like magic how it lifts it up off the floor. It's kind of hard to steer, but you can go all the way from one end of the warehouse to the other, and even give your brother rides. But the forklift is an actual vehicle, so I can't drive it alone, and no one should ride it. I'm also not allowed to drive the reach truck, which is a forklift that goes all the way to the top pallet racking. And I can't push the button on the cardboard baler because if a child got in there without anyone knowing, they would die. It would be really horrible if they got flattened in there like in a James Bond movie. It would crunch all their bones and I'm sure blood would seep out the bottom. I don't know who these children would be since Chris and I are the only people ever there on weekends, but I can throw boxes in for recycling if I flatten them first and as long as I'm supervised by a grown-up.

I'm going to get a car in four years when I turn 16, but I have to earn the money. I know some people borrow their parents' cars and some people get a car for a birthday present, but in my family, we earn our own money. It will

probably be American made, maybe a Ford. Most families
choose one or the other. Ford or General Motors and Coke
or Pepsi and Crest or Colgate and Republican or Democrat.
It takes a lot of stapling and stuffing envelopes to earn a car.
I babysit a lot too. You can watch TV or do homework when
you're babysitting, after the children go to sleep. "Love Boat"
comes on first, and then "Fantasy Island," and usually then
the parents come home. I charge $1 per hour. I never fall
asleep on the couch, but I don't like it if the people stay out
till "Saturday Night Live" is on, because I know my parents
will be at home watching it in their bedroom and laughing,
and I feel kind of lonely to be in someone else's house then,
even though I don't watch it with my parents. I usually don't
know why they're laughing so much. I guess I'm too young
for adult humor.

   I like to stay in my room and read Nancy Drew Mysteries
late at night, and I like hearing my parents laughing in their
bedroom at the same time. I have 23 Nancy Drew books so
far, about half of them from my grandma. She writes me a
little note in the front before she wraps them. She said she
likes to give me books for presents because then I'll think of
her as I'm reading them. Sometimes she even reads them
first, so we can talk about the stories in our letters. My
favorite Nancy Drew is number two, *The Hidden Staircase*. I
like stairs. I dream about stairs a lot. Concrete stairs, metal
stairs like the mezzanine at the warehouse, stairs up to a
bridge over a river, guarded by a Vietnamese soldier. That's a
weird dream I keep having. Sometimes he's nice, sometimes
he's the enemy. The stinky stairwell in my mom's friend's
New York apartment building. Red painted wooden stairs
like the back stairs to where Barley's bed is. But that's not
why *The Hidden Staircase* is my favorite Nancy Drew. That's
just a coincidence.

   My name is kind of like Nancy Drew. I wish we spelled
Drue like Drew. Sometimes I think I'd like to be a sleuth like

Nancy Drew and her friends George and Bess. "Sleuth" means detective. They're all smart girls, but Nancy is the leader and she solves the mysteries, and she's the one I would be.

34. Tiny Bread Crust

I don't mind going to chapel and saying the Lord's Prayer and learning some Bible things, because I love the stained glass windows in there, red and purple with the light behind them, and the dark wooden beams in the ceiling, and the wooden pews all lined up and the needle-pointed covers on the kneelers that you pull down on a hinge for everybody to kneel at the right time. It feels like you're in a ship. They don't usually do communion because it takes too long, and chapel is just during the school day twice a week, so we can't take too much time for it. But we have done it a few times and every time, Reverend Chase says you have to be baptized to take communion. So I don't go up, and I always feel a little sad and lonely when everyone else goes up. Mom says if it's that big a deal I can go and get myself baptized whatever religion I want. When I type those words, it sounds like she was being nice, but trust me, it was sarcastic. Whenever you're in doubt if your mom or your friend is being sarcastic, it's best to assume they are.

But yesterday in chapel Reverend Chase gave us a piece of bread, like a one-inch square of bread crust as if it was for communion, and everybody got it no matter who they were. He brought the basket to our pew instead of calling us up front and said everyone should take one. Maybe he forgot I was there and I'm not baptized, but I was happy I could finally eat a piece of communion bread, even though I think it was just Wonder Bread, same as on my peanut-butter-and-jelly sandwich upstairs in my lunch box, and my piece of communion bread wasn't even very good because it was crust. I was really hungry. I don't think communion bread, even if it's specially made with the help of God and it's supposed to be part of the body of Jesus Christ (which seems pretty gross, to be honest), helps with hunger unless it's a miracle. And if it's real, certifiable hunger like on the news in Africa, it would take a really big miracle.

But chapel lasted 45 minutes so I decided to make the tiny bread crust last as long as I could. I took little bites off of it, so small you could almost not feel it on your tongue. I pretended I was one of the Jews starving to death in a concentration camp and that was my only food. We said the Lord's Prayer at the end, and I still had a crumb left from that piece of bread.

"Our father who art in Heaven, hallowed be thy name..."

It didn't fill me up though. My stomach felt hallowed, which might not be the right use of that word. Hollow. If I was in a concentration camp, I would die if that was my only food, but it did fill the time all through chapel, like another kind of miracle.

35. Up for Grabs

U sually lunch is PBJ and a smiley face on my napkin. Maybe carrot sticks or an apple or something else I don't eat. If someone gets potato chips they don't want, like Billy Whitaker, he stands on a chair and holds them up over his head and yells "up for grabs." Everyone goes and jumps for it. The boys, anyway. I usually don't want anything that's up for grabs.

My favorite lunch is when my mom puts a hot dog in a thermos of boiling water, so the hot dog is cooked and all nice and warm, and the water has cooled down just enough and gets kind of salty from the hot dog so you can drink it like soup. If anyone lifted that up for grabs, I might try to jump, but I'm pretty sure my mom is the only one who does hot dogs this way.

I think she got the hot dog idea from a book on how to be a good mom. One of her favorite books is by Dr. Spock. His book says when your child is bad, you should criticize your child's actions but not your child. A good mom would say "stealing money from my purse was very bad" instead of saying "you are a very bad girl." That seems pretty smart, but my mom probably shouldn't have told me, because now if I know Dr. Spock's secrets, I'm not sure they'll work on me anymore. For any good trick to work, the parent (or teacher or policeman or magician) should be aware of the whole thing, and the regular person (or child) has to be a little in the dark. Mom also said she learned it would be good if Chris and I are both mad at her or afraid of her at the same time. If she is our common enemy, my brother and I will become close friends. I don't like that tip because we're already friends, and couldn't we find a better common enemy, and not have to be afraid of our own mom?

We do have a secret hiding place though, on the third floor. It's in the back of the closet and there's only room for the two of us. I put a flashlight up there already. If either of us gets scared enough, we just tell the other, and we'll both go up there to hide. That's our deal. If either of us says we have to go there, we will drop everything and go.

36. Library Books

Constance reads a lot, and our moms let us go to the library on the public bus, as long as we go straight there and straight back with our books and I walk her halfway home from the bus stop, so neither of us has to be alone any longer than the other one. Well, my mom wouldn't mind if I walk alone because I can look after myself, like I know if a car slows down next to you, turn around and run the opposite way. But Constance is better off with a friend because of her mom being La Mouse the Model, and Constance looks like her mom, which sometimes gives people bad ideas. Constance's younger sister Sabine looks more like their dad, black hair and eyebrows that almost meet in the middle, and pretty big muscles for a girl, so I don't think she would have the same kind of problems in public. Still, they don't let her go on the public bus since she's only ten. My mom says Sabine will probably be beautiful when she's older, and she will pluck her eyebrows with tweezers, which seems like it would sting. You can check out eight library books for two weeks.

Sometimes I talk to the librarians or read the bulletin board. Constance always goes straight to the bookshelves. She reads the back and front and author's name and everything she can find. Sometimes she has already read a certain book and she tells me I would like it. She's usually right, except for *A Wrinkle in Time*, which I didn't really like. Also, *The Secret Garden*. But every other book she tells me about, I love. Especially *From the Mixed Up Files of Mrs. Basil E. Frankweiler*. You can imagine you are in that book, living with your brother at the Metropolitan Museum in New York. I would pick that book to live in even if my other choice would be a Nancy Drew.

Every time, we both check out the limit. That's a lot of books to bring home on a bus, especially for me because I know I will only read maybe three at the most because I like to go to the pool and play with my brother and play outside. But Constance finishes her whole stack every time, usually the first week of our two weeks, and then she walks to my house in one of her light pink dresses and knee socks and penny loafers, or we meet halfway to trade what we already read. By then I might have only read one or two, but at least she gets one or two extras that way. She is the fastest reader I know. Sometimes we quiz her to see if she really reads the stories. And she always does.

If you don't believe your friend who says they did something, you can test them. If it turns out they were lying, just let it go. But if it turns out they were telling the truth, you better tell everyone and make a big deal about it because it really is a big deal, and you were the mean one who doubted it. And you should probably have her over for at least three sleepovers to make up for it. You can tell a lot about your friends from how they make up for their mistakes.

37. Conveyor Belt

On Monday afternoons, Constance comes with me to do stapling and projects at my dad's company, and we both get a dollar an hour. We have done four Mondays but I don't know if she wants to keep working there because we also have homework to do on Mondays, and she's not saving up for something special like I am. Probably if she wants money in high school, she'll become a model like her mom La Mouse, who went to Paris when she was only seventeen. Models can make a ton of money, but you have to be skinny and young and pretty of course. The problem with a job like that is you might always be skinny and pretty, but you're not going to stay young, so modeling can only work out for so long. Business is a much better bet. The more experienced you are, the smarter you will be, and you'll make more friends and colleagues as you go along, so your business will just keep getting better. I like working Saturdays more than Mondays because I can be there all day and get more done and more money.

Here's a poem I wrote yesterday when Chris and I went to the warehouse to staple statement stuffers for the invoices. There were three sheets of paper about towels this time, with black-and-white pictures. Color pictures would probably be better, so people would want to buy the towels for their stores, but color brochures take longer and it's expensive so you might not have a good return on investment. It's too bad though, because they are really nice, colorful towels to match anybody's bathroom, and I think customers might like to see all the colors instead of just read their names. Lilac. Canary yellow. Avocado. Mint green. Peach. Peacock Blue. Aubergine. Aubergine is the fancy French way to say eggplant. That has to be the dumbest color ever because in a towel it's purple, but in real life it's black. When my mom makes eggplant slices as a side dish, they're slimy! No one wants to eat them, not even my dad, and he is normally enthusiastic about his vegetables.

The best towels are 100% cotton from Egypt, with extra large terry loops, which are the most absorbent. Chris bangs his stapler, but I gently push, and by the end of the day, I do more stapling, so his way isn't faster even though it seems like it might be. And also, sometimes he breaks the stapler. We both hate paper cuts!

Conveyor Belt
by Sandy Drue

I want to lie
on the conveyor belt
in a nice brown box
with magic air holes
that are invisible.
No shrink wrap
no stretch wrap
no fiber bands.
I just go round
and round the warehouse
with my knees up in my cozy box
till someone hauls me off,
takes me home,
and unpacks me.

Poems don't have to rhyme! I am going to write a book someday and this poem will go in my book, and all the stories I take home to my Miss Piggy box. Jessamyn Hart made my Miss Piggy box for my birthday two years ago, and only very special things go in it. If you keep all your stories and poems, you can go back later and change your writing if you want – which is called editing – or if you learned how to spell something that you didn't know before, you can fix it. I like to draw, so I might illustrate my book too. I don't know yet. Some people say only children's books have pictures, and I want to write a real book.

But even if you don't plan to write a book, you might want to keep the stuff you write because they're like letters from your younger self to the future you. You never know – even if you have lots of friends today, you might move or they might move, or for some other reason, you might be very lonely someday, and it will be nice to have such a good friend who knows you so well there in those letters writing to you. My Miss Piggy mailbox is probably the one thing I would take with me in a fire. I keep one birthday card from John in there, one from Joy, and one special letter from my grandma. If you're prepared, there probably will never be a fire. Also, if you bring your umbrella, it probably won't rain. That's the opposite of Murphy's Law, which says if something can possibly go wrong, it will. I'm saying if you prepare for it to go wrong, it won't. I like my personal version of Murphy better!

I do like using my dad's electric typewriters on Saturdays, but I don't like the front office because the carpet is horrible goldenrod with a pattern in it like big cobblestones gouged out with a u-shaped rubber-stamp knife. And front office people leave their cigarettes in their ashtrays which smell terrible. No wonder Mom's whole department is upstairs on the Mezzanine with cool music and posters and a leather Chesterfield sofa for her artists to lie down and cogitate. But it's worth it to be in the front office because of the typewriters. Also, there's always paper, including carbon paper, so you get two copies at once. One for Miss Piggy and one to mail to your grandmother in Florida. Just don't get carbon paper on your clothes because that purple ink doesn't wash out. You can re-use one sheet of carbon paper, and re-using supplies is smart for your business, but not too many times or it stops working. Things that don't work right are bad for your business!

When my mom was little she wrote a newspaper which I have at home. Here's my favorite poem from her newspaper, which I have memorized, but I don't think she wrote it. It's kind of old-fashioned, and it makes her laugh her head off if I say it. If you write fiction, you have to write your own words, but if you are a newspaper reporter, you write what other people say, and you have to get their words exactly right if you quote them.

Little Willy in the best of sashes
Fell in the fire and was burnt to ashes
Even though the room got chilly,
No one wanted to poke up Willy.

Today they don't usually name a boy Willy, and no boys wear sashes. I imagine little Willy's sash was light blue satin, which would be very silly on a boy today.

38. Favorite Socks

Since I'm talking about poems, I'll tell you about my favorite socks. They are not my toe socks, like some people might think. I don't actually like toe socks because I think toes are supposed to be together. Toe socks are uncomfortable and your feet look weird like stubby hands in gloves. Toe socks are unnatural!

My favorite socks are normal white knee socks with printing, and actually, they're not so white anymore, but you can still see the printing. And maybe it's not a poem, technically, it's an advertising jingle on my socks. The words go all the way up to my knee. You can guess what it is:

Two all
beef
patties
special
sauce
lettuce
cheese
pickles
onions
on a
sesame
seed bun

and then there's a picture of it at my ankle. A Big Mac!

39. A Good Shot

Guns and camping and driving a Winnebago are all normal for Aunt Lula and Uncle Frank but not my mom because my mom is a New Yorker, and my parents are city people. They like museums and shows and department store windows, and they say the way to win a battle is with a mean wit. Not fists or violence or bullets, which is for peasants. "Peasants" is a good insult because there's no such thing as peasants anymore so you won't really insult anyone innocent by accident when you say it. I hope I'll be smart enough to have a mean wit when I'm an adult, even though I'm not growing up in New York like my mom did. For now I'd rather just fit in where I am. I go to camp and swim and ride a horse and muck out the stalls. I'm not afraid of holding a snake, and I like fishing although I don't like to clean my own fish when I catch one. But I'm a pretty good shot with a .22 rifle. Even though you are actually a "shooter" if you shoot a gun, you should call yourself "a good shot" to prove you know the lingo.

I squeeze the trigger smooth and slow, that's the trick, and don't hold your breath but breathe slow and shallow through it when you squeeze. I learned the word "prone" from riflery, which means lying down on your stomach when you shoot. You can aim the gun and hold it steady when you're prone. "Supine" also means lying down, but it's lying on your back, so it's pretty useless for riflery, unless you're shooting at the sky, I guess.

I like shooting the rifle. When we're done, everyone puts their safety on and guns down, and we tromp along the gravel to the far end, and it smells so good in there, and we unclip our targets. One bullet hole for every shot. Sometimes even a bull's-eye. Sometimes there are two holes touching or maybe even three like a snowman! Or maybe you missed the paper, and there's no hole for one of your bullets – but *maybe* it went straight through one of your other holes! How would you ever know? I love the crack-sound and straight line of every shot. I wouldn't love a machine gun because that's for war and enemies and too much action and chaos. And I wouldn't love a shot gun. Bullets should go straight and true at their target, not all scattershot. Unless I guess you're not so clear on what your target is. You might not be lucky enough to be shooting in a rifle range. Not everything in the whole wide world can be precise.

I love the black and brass smell of the hot empty bullet shells and the cool, dark rifle range when it's bright and sunny outside. I got a letter of congratulations and Junior Membership from the National Rifle Association, which my mother says makes her horrified, but she framed it anyway and hung it on the wall. She said raising me and Chris here is like hosting foreign exchange students who never go home.

I want to be a foreign exchange student. I want every page in my passport to have stamps in it. I want my parents to host students from Brazil and Australia and Switzerland and Scotland and Spain. Maybe even Russia! I want to learn a lot of languages. Hola. Konichiwa. Obrigado. Shalom. I want to be a girl no one expects to speak a really rare language and then there's an emergency and no one knows what the person is saying and suddenly I'm the one who's fluent.

40. Kitchen Cabinets

Want to know how to say kitchen cabinets in Swiss German? It's "who-he-hash-lee." That's not how you spell it, but you don't need to know how to spell it because they don't write their words in Swiss German anyway. The German from Germany is called High German, and they call a kitchen cabinet a *kuchenschrank*. They speak German in Austria too. There's a Swiss lady who comes to all the trade shows and she's my favorite vendor. She and her husband sell belts. She's from Lucerne, so she taught me "who-he-hash-lee." I wish her name was Heidi, because she has long blond hair that she wears in a braid sometimes, and she really seems like a Heidi, but her name is plain old Anne, like Anne from Anywhere. She lets me call her Mrs. Anne instead of Mrs. So-and-so because her surname is very long and hard to pronounce. She calls her last name a surname because that's what they say in Europe. We call her husband Mr. Joaquim, which isn't so easy to say in itself. You pronounce his "J" like a "w."

I plan to never forget "who-he-hash-lee" not because I think I'll need it, but just because I like the sound of it, and I like Mrs. Anne and all her belts. She has silver elastic belts with metal buckles that loop together like a figure eight, and looking at those buckles sort of reminds me of the sound of "who-he-hash-lee." Even when you hear the metal buckle parts slide into place, it sounds like "who-he-hash-lee" in my mind. Even though the Swiss Germans supposedly don't write their words down, Mrs. Anne wrote it for me in red pen. You would never pronounce it right just from looking at it. *Chuchichaschtli.* See what I mean? I put her note in my Miss Piggy mailbox so I'd remember to write a little story about it. Anything you want to remember needs its special place.

I have a favorite word in Turkish too. *Yakamoz.* It means the reflection of the moon on water, when it moves, like because of the wind or waves or little paddles or fish swimming near the surface. Just imagining that black with silver water makes me happy. Mr. Shafak is Turkish and he sells shoes. Well, he's Turkish-American, I mean. And Mrs. Anne and Mr. Joaquim are Swiss-American, because they all immigrated to America, and they live in New York. All their belts and shoes and everything we buy is made in America! At least we try to only buy American, but it's getting harder because the foreign stuff is good and cheap. The government is trying to make it harder to buy the foreign stuff with taxes but Dad says it's a losing battle.

Mr. Shafak usually has his display next to Mrs. Anne's belts, and he heard us talking about words, and that's why he taught me *yakamoz.* He said Turkish is the most beautiful language in the world, but I think that's like my dad saying my mom is the most beautiful woman in the world. People probably always love their own wives and words and ways of doing things the most. Mrs. Anne agreed with him though because she is Swiss and so she says it's in her nature to be neutral. I put *yakamoz* in the box too.

I also have a cigar box full of hockey ticket stubs, from the Scouts, Blues, and Red Wings, and another box of Charlie's Angels cards, that will be collectors' items if I ever need to sell them. I have a Hummel figurine for the same reason, only I dropped it so I don't think it'll ever sell for very much money. Plus, when I want to sell it, maybe no one will collect Hummels.

I also have a white jewelry box with a plastic ballerina that twirls in a mirror, and it plays music when you open the lid. Every single girl I know has that same jewelry box, and we twang the ballerina on her spring. It's easy to break the ballerina though. Most of my friends' ballerinas are missing because they got twanged off.

Constance taught me how to say *illigitimi non carborundum* which is Latin for "don't let the bastards get you down." We are going to take Latin next year. If you know Latin, it can help you get into a good college. "Bastard" is a bad word in English, but when you think about what it means, it's ridiculous. It's not like it's up to you whether your parents were married to each other when you were born or not, so obviously you don't deserve some rude accusation like bastard. If I ran the world, I'd get rid of the word bastard. (Well, no I wouldn't because I believe in free speech and studying history so it doesn't repeat itself). But I don't get why it's so terrible for two people to have a baby without being married, just because that's not how it's usually done. Of course it's nice for children to grow up with two parents who love them and love each other and are nice people, but marriage is just a piece of paper. Babies are innocent! Why do so many insults seem to target the wrong person? Also, God's not mean! If He exists, I don't think he gives a monkey's butt about bastards.

Not everyone in high school likes Latin. Here's what they say: "Latin is a language, dead as it can be. First it killed the Romans, now it's killing me." I'm not scared though. A lot of history is related to Latin, like *e pluribus unum* which is "out of many comes one" about the United States. I think that's the best thing ever, and why I'm proud to be American, even though they could have just said it in English and not tried to be so fancy in Latin. The United States is a melting pot, and that's not fancy. If it was supposed to be fancy, you'd call it a chafing dish.

41. No Shoes All Summer

Sarah Fitzgerald is my favorite summer friend because Chris and I can go to their house every day that we don't go to camp and we never have to wear shoes because they're on the same block, and no one has to cross any streets. You should wear shoes if you cross a street. I don't know why.

Only one problem – Sarah is kind of creepy in love with Holly Hobby. Holly Hobby wallpaper, Holly Hobby doll, Holly Hobby lunch box, Holly Hobby bedspread. She said she'd change her name to Holly Hobby if she could, but luckily, I don't think you can change your name without your parents' permission until you're eighteen. Maybe Mrs. Fitzgerald would let Sarah change it sooner. She's obviously the one who did the wallpaper and everything. Just because someone's a mom, doesn't mean they always have good judgment or good taste. But other than the Holly Hobby business, I like Sarah.

Sarah's brother Steve plays with Chris, and we even bring Barley to play with their dog Rocky sometimes. We just have to be home by 6pm. That's the only rule. And one more thing, we cannot cut anyone's hair including Sarah's dolls. We got in big trouble for that once because it was a fancy doll – a collectible one that was no longer collectible after its haircut. Sarah is younger than me, but she already has hair on her private parts. She showed me in the bathroom because I didn't believe her. I hate the word pubic. Maybe it's natural, but I think it's a gross word, and it bothered me to even write that word, but now I will never say it, write it, or type it again unless for some reason I have to.

They have lots of games in Sarah's house and good outside toys, like a playhouse, swing set with a slide, bikes and trikes and a big wheel, and their mom lets us do other fun stuff inside, sometimes even cooking.

Sarah's mom said we could make sugar cookies if we could do it ourselves, and we had to promise to share with Chris and Steve. My mom hates cooking, so I was excited to do it at Sarah's house. Sugar cookies are my third favorites, and snickerdoodles are my second favorites because they have cinnamon, which I love. In Sweden they eat cinnamon in winter because it puts them in a good mood. You have to be careful about things that put you in a good mood, like cigarettes for instance, because it could be innocent enough, but it might be a gateway to something dangerous, like in *Go Ask Alice*, where she ends up addicted to drugs. I think cinnamon really is innocent though, and not a gateway. In *Go Ask Alice*, she accidentally has LSD because someone puts it in her drink and then she gets totally out of control and runs away from home and has to write her diary on paper towels. Finally, mostly because she got in with a really bad crowd, she can't stop doing drugs, and she dies.

That story is true and it has nothing to do with snickerdoodles, but it just seemed important to mention how easily things can get out of control. Sometimes important lessons just come up when they come up, and you have to just accept that, the timing might not be perfect, but the lesson is what really matters. I would never do LSD or have friends who would put it in my drink, because if you do it once, it can keep on making you hallucinate, even years later. That would be terrible. Things that happened in the past need to stay in the past unless you specifically want them to come along into the future with you.

My top favorite cookie is chocolate chip with no chocolate chips. Just the cookie part. It's almost impossible to get. Someday if someone wants to prove they love me, they will bake chocolate chip cookies for me with no chips. But no one ever believes I truly like them that way, so they will probably always add the chips. My mom says I should not assume no one will ever love me, because everyone can find love if they look in the right places and let it find them if they go to the right places. The trick is to go to those places and stay still long enough to get found.

I don't know why she says stuff like that though, because deep down I think the boy I love might love me back, even though he doesn't say anything about it because he's kind of shy.

In *Go Ask Alice*, the thing with the LSD in their drinks was a finding game they called "Button, Button, Who's Got the Button?" which sounds like a nursery rhyme, and just proves that something you think might be innocent could actually be very dangerous.

When Sarah and I made the sugar cookies, we followed the recipe, and when they were done, they looked perfect, but they tasted like earwax. I said maybe they were poisoned. Sarah's mom checked all our ingredients, and it turned out we used Worcestershire sauce instead of vanilla, so we had to throw them away. Then Chris and Barley and I had to go home, and it was like we threw away a whole day.

42. Pokey Thing

A recipe works best if you actually follow it. If you're a good cook with lots of experience, maybe you only need the written recipe as a reminder, but the written record should make it possible to do the thing the right way. Or at least it will tell you how it's done by all the people who follow that recipe. That's why it's best to write down plans and promises, especially in business. They say "get it in writing," and then it's called a contract.

Chris and I have to submit invoices for our allowance. "Submit" means turn in or give someone something. It's important in business to use the right words for things so people trust you. We don't have to write all the chores we did on our invoice, even though we are supposed to make our beds every day and put dirty clothes in the laundry and put clean clothes away, set the table, and load and empty the dishwasher. If we submit an invoice, our dad trusts us that we did our jobs. Sometimes we don't do them, but if there's a good reason, like Chris was at soccer practice and he couldn't set the table or something, that's OK. When we submit our invoice, it has to have our name at the top and the date and that's all. We put in on his desk, and when he pays us, he writes "paid" on it, and he jabs it on his pokey thing. I know there is a real name for the pokey thing, which is like a spike or a really long skinny nail poking through a wooden disk. It's kind of old-fashioned and I don't think many businesses use pokey things anymore, but I know I should still find out its name.

We get more money from working than from allowance, but we still never want to forget to get our allowance. Mom and Dad say we have to submit invoices so we'll learn how to run a business, but I think it's only because they can never remember if they paid us.

43. Bad Luck, Good Luck

My dad says bad luck is just bad luck. Good luck is just good luck. But he also says people make their own luck. If you work really hard and you're smart, you will make your own good luck. I think Thomas Jefferson said something like that first, and it's good to give credit to our founding fathers when they deserve it, and considering he wrote the Declaration of Independence, he was obviously a pretty important writer. But my dad said it first to me, in his own way, so it's my dad's quote as far as I'm concerned. My dad also says if you do stupid things, you'll probably make your own bad luck. But people don't get cancer or diabetes or have a baby with Down syndrome as any kind of punishment. People who believe that are very "limited," which is a polite way to say they're stupid. For people as stupid as that, though I'd rather just call them stupid.

You know that Golden Rule that might be Confucius' golden rule, treat other people as you'd like to be treated yourself? I think you should also think about people as you'd like to be thought of yourself, because whether you like it or not, what you think about a person always comes out in your actions. You can always find something to like in everyone, even if it's hard to focus on that one thing when there's a lot you don't like.

My dad also says there are no secret, spiritual messages from the universe guiding people. A weird thing is just a coincidence, which, if you want to be silly, you can call a "co-inky-dink." I think my dad calls it a co-inky-dink in his silly voice because he doesn't like not being able to explain it, and people use funny accents and silly words when they feel uncomfortable. People still have a lot to learn about modern medicine and science, and not understanding something is uncomfortable. Like back when they put leeches on people to suck out their bad blood, that was because their knowledge was limited. And they thought if a girl could swim she was a witch. I'm glad I didn't live back then, because I love to swim, and if they threw me in the water to test me, I would swim away. Then when they caught me, they would think I was a witch and they'd have to burn me to death, which would be a terrible way to go. A lot worse than drowning, in fact.

Leeches are different though. I think leeches might have worked because even though they really were sucking the person's blood out, there could have been the placebo effect. A placebo is when you give someone a fake pill but you tell them it is a very effective cure, and they take it, and they believe it, so suddenly they are cured. That's called "mind over matter," and there are lots of examples of it working in science and modern medicine. And just because we don't understand something, doesn't make it not true.

I think my dad understands more about the world and what people are willing to believe because of his magic shows. I like knowing he's a magician, but I don't want to know all the tricks, because then a placebo pill wouldn't work on me. I would know it was just a trick, and then the leeches couldn't cure me and I would die.

I guess I should tell you my grandma has cancer. I said maybe it will go away, like the tumor could disappear like you hear on the news sometimes. But she said her plan to take me to Rome for my 16th birthday probably won't work out now. I told her I think it still will. It's only four years away, and people can live with cancer for many years, especially if they think positive. I know she wants to be the one to show me Rome, but it kind of seems like she's planning to die first, and she isn't thinking very positive.

I'm not sure what my mom thinks is going to happen. Every time I think about my mom knowing her mom might die, I start to cry. So I've been trying not to think about it except for positive thinking like Zig Ziglar on my dad's tapes. He's good at making people keep a positive attitude. I wish Grandma would listen to Zig Ziglar. I told her that on the phone and she said, "fooey," which made everybody laugh on all our separate phone extensions. So even without meaning to, Zig Ziglar made her feel positive for just a minute.

44. Mail

There are lots of ways to talk to someone you can't be with. You can mail her a letter. You can call on the phone. You can write them a message and not even mail it, and they still will kind of know you were thinking of them, even if they don't know what your message was, exactly. You can even just think of them and they might feel good like *oh, someone cares about me.* That's how a lot of people talk to God, only silently in their heads and not even on their knees, with their hands in the old-fashioned praying style, and you still can call it praying, when you talk to God that way, just in your head. Mom says Trudie has a direct line to God, and I should ask her what religion I should be, so I did. She was ironing napkins. She said, "Oh honey, the words you choose don't matter, or the place you're standing, when you talk to God. He hears you no matter what. Even if you don't quite know what you're asking, He knows. You just start talking in your own mind." I put my hand on the hot, smooth napkin stack. We only use fabric napkins for a dinner party. They feel good. I said, "And He answers?" Trudie said, "In His way." She laughed a little in her nice quiet way that you know she's just happy and never making fun of you. She stood the iron up on end and said, "It's a mystery. He hears you, honey, and answers come."

I liked what Trudie said, how no matter how you're asking a thing, He hears it. If He's real, I mean.

I kind of hope He is. Or She. Or It. Because God is an

idea, so It doesn't have a gender. People like to think of God as a person, and we like our people to be male or female, and look like we do, so we know how to relate to them. Like if you have a teacher who's a woman you might behave a little differently than with your teacher who's a man. We are all different with Mr. Islington our science teacher, but I don't think it's because he's a man. It's because he hits us with his ruler, and he has a snake that got loose in the classroom, and sometimes he has a beard and sometimes he shaves it off, so I feel like he can't be trusted. Camille says you can't make demands for God to prove His existence to you. You can only ask yourself to have faith. I would never want to try to bully God or anything, but if He is real, why couldn't He just say so somehow, to the people like me who might be just a little on the fence? Because it seems to me He could be real and modern science can also be real, even if when you think about it in a scientific way, the science seems easier to prove.

Even if God's an It, you should capitalize the "I" in It, because It's the most important thing in the whole universe. The only other word you always capitalize besides proper names like Sandy and Chris and New York and Miami and so on would be President for President of the United States of America. That's the most important job in our country. But it's just a tiny thing compared to God. President is only for four years, and half the people don't even respect him. God is forever, that's the whole point of God, and everyone who believes in God respects Him or Her or It.

Also, if you're dying of a fatal illness and a doctor knows how to save you, he or she would be much more important in that moment than the President. But if you're dying of a fatal illness, you might think God would be even more important than the doctor. Or you can think they're both important. Don't forget to capitalize the D in "Dr" like for Dr. Clayton. It's a proper name, and also, it's important.

My grandma's doctor is an oncologist, which is a cancer

doctor. We are going to visit her soon to try to cheer her up. Spring Break used to be called Easter Break, but then they changed it so it wouldn't be offensive. They still call Christmas Break Christmas Break though, and for some reason no one gets offended by that. Maybe because Christmas Break is always during Christmas whereas Spring Break is sometimes not during Easter. I'm a little nervous about seeing my grandma because my mom says she's not herself, and I don't know what that means. I know she can't play Frisbee with me like usual, but I don't think my mom knows exactly what it means either. But it must be upsetting because there are a lot of times their bedroom door is closed, and my parents always seem to be talking very quietly with serious faces.

45. Painting Your Dog's Nails

You might have a dog who's so nice he'll let you paint his toenails, but don't forget he won't actually like it. You are doing it for your own fun. If you paint a little girl's toenails or fingernails, she usually likes it, and that's fun for both of you, as long as her mom doesn't mind. But not dogs. Dogs like a walk, a ball, or rolling over to get a belly rub. If you do that stuff for him, he will love you. It's true for people too. If you want someone to love you, you have to do what they like to do and hopefully you like it too. If you want someone to love you and you hate all the things they like to do, then I recommend you find a different person to love.

If you don't want to ever give your dog a belly rub, you're probably just not a dog person, and that's OK. Not everybody is. I would never try to paint Barley's nails, but he does let me put a rubber band around his nose sometimes. It's pretty funny watching him try to get it off. I bet he wishes he had opposable thumbs.

46. You Can't Practice for Someone Dying

Everybody is going to die. It's just a fact and there's nothing you can do about it, like to prepare for when they die. That's what I'm trying to say. It's not like gymnastics where you get better every time you swing yourself up on the uneven bars, so by the time you have to actually do a pull-over in front of people, you can do it. And it's not like reading a sad book, you know – a tragedy – and feeling tragic or reading a scary book or seeing a scary movie and feeling terrified. It feels like the same emotion, but it's not the same as when it's real.

Grief is really bad sadness and you can't practice to get better at it. Nobody wants to get good at grief. Anyone who is going through grief is allowed to go through it in their own way and they are automatically as good at it as they ever need to be. So my advice is try not to worry about it before it happens.

My first newspaper article for school was on a movie about a man dying, and when the doctors told him he was going to die, he went through all the stages of grief: denial, (no way, this can't be happening) anger, (NO WAY!), bargaining, (no, don't take me, take that guy I hate, or maybe if I promise to eat my broccoli every night, let me live), depression (you know what this is... it's like really pathetic sadness that probably makes you not say anything or see anybody and not even want to get out of bed), acceptance (like OK, I guess I really am dying, which is a shame, but I guess I'll just get on with it).

I don't know if those stages of grief for the guy dying are the same stages if someone you love is dying, but I'm sure they're both grief.

For example, you might think "my grandma is going to die someday and I will be really sad, maybe so sad I will never recover from my sadness." You might think you can have small bits of sadness over a longer period of time, starting now, to make it not so awful at the time – like go through the first stage or two ahead of time. Like if you learn to read and write before first grade, you'll be ahead of the class, which is nice when you're six or seven years old, but that kind of thing doesn't work with grown-up problems like people dying. If you try to be sad when she's still alive, it's not real, and you're going to waste your time that you could have been enjoying with her.

I don't know what happens to a person after they die. I mean, their body is dead of course, but I mean their "them." I guess no one can know for sure until it happens to them, and by then it's too late to let the rest of us know. Maybe someday a scientist will solve that riddle and find a way to get some answers. Although, then other scientists will probably call that first scientist a crackpot and ruin his career. Scientists don't really want to think about whether or not there's an afterlife, because it's impossible to prove.

47. Advice from Chris

I asked Chris, do you have any advice to put in my book? And he said if you're ever attacked by a bully, just laugh.

I have never tested this advice myself. It might just be for boys. But it still could be good to know, as a last resort.

Actually, the rape lecture people at school said you should sing nursery rhymes like "Mary Had a Little Lamb" and laugh and drool and try to vomit, and then your rapist might think something is terribly wrong with you and be so disturbed he'll leave you alone. Also, you should carry your car keys in your hand, poking through your fingers to make a weapon and don't walk through dark parking lots alone at night. I will have to remember to have a lot of keys.

48. Elevator Pervert

Maybe this is a good place to tell you some advice from my mom, even though it's not supposed to be for my book, it's just advice that's good to know. In any big city, it's important to have street smarts, especially in New York. Really, you should have street smarts no matter where you are. You can get bad grades in school because you're not smart in that way, but if you have street smarts, that's much more important. For instance, if a man exposes himself to you in front of an elevator, look him in the eye and say "you should be ashamed of yourself," and then quickly walk away. Don't ever ride the elevator with him or with anyone who gives you the creeps. I think I mentioned that already, but it's important!

This is what my mom's friend did one time when she was little. It might be even smarter though just to get away from the man and don't try to teach him a lesson.

In case you don't know, it's kind of silly, but that phrase "exposes himself" means he shows you his penis. The problem is there are some men called perverts who like to show their private parts to little girls, and if you do the wrong thing when they show you, they might kidnap you and kill you. But mostly, that will never happen, so there's no need to worry about it.

49. Slumber Parties

There are a few things that are part of every slumber party. First of all, a slumber party is a sleepover with at least two friends at another friend's house, and you have to sleep in sleeping bags, not in beds. If it's only one friend at another friend's house, that's just a sleepover, even if you sleep on the floor. A slumber party is good for turning nine years old. Before then you will almost always end up with certain girls crying and maybe having to go home. Later than age nine is fine, but you'll start to feel a little old for it and some girls will want to do stupid and dangerous things as you get older, like with neighborhood boys. That's the trouble with outgrowing things that used to be fun – people try to add in stupid and dangerous things to make the old traditional ones fun again.

1. Tell ghost stories. This is a good way to get everybody in the right mood for scary stuff. It's best if you sit in a circle in a dark room. If it's not dark outside yet, like because it's summer, then just make sure it's dark. You should be in your pajamas already. Then whoever tells the story holds a flashlight under their chin (pointing at the ceiling) while they talk. I personally think the flashlight trick is weird and not scary, but it's tradition. The best ghost stories always end with some shock like the bad guy is in your house. It's OK to tell ghost stories everyone has heard before. People will still like the way you tell it.

2. Truth or Dare. I don't recommend this game. Anyone who picks "truth" never has any secrets to tell. If she does, she will regret telling it at a slumber party, and teachers will get involved later, and someone always gets in trouble – almost always, the wrong person. Anyone who picks "dare" probably secretly wants to sneak into your friend's brother's room, or go in the garage naked, or run out to the street in a Lady Godiva wig, or whatever you dare her to do. Basically, just don't encourage girls like that. Also, if you climb ladders in nightgowns, that's dangerous, and naked stuff is always dangerous.

3. Bloody Mary. This one kind of freaks people out. Everyone gets in front of a mirror and it's dark. The flashlight points at the person in the front. At the same time, everyone chants "Bloody Mary" 50 times, and then she will appear in the mirror. There's some kind of history lesson about the Queen of England who got beheaded, probably one of King Henry the Eighth's wives, because he had seven wives and they got: divorced, beheaded, died, divorced, beheaded, survived. (Although that actually only adds up to six wives, so maybe I'm wrong). Usually someone gets bored by about 25 at the most, but depending on who's at your party, maybe they'll go all the way to fifty. I told people I saw her once, and then I actually believed it myself even though I'm pretty sure I made it up. She had a long, red and black dress with ruffles and black hair piled on her head and big red flower behind her ear and black dance shoes, and she was spinning and dancing, holding the hem of her ruffled dress up by her hip. There was no sound, only the lady dancing in the mirror. It was probably totally fake because the Henry the Eighth thing would mean Bloody Mary should

be English, and that lady I saw was pretty Spanish-y. The reason it's scary is people say if you see her then someone will die in their sleep or they'll never be able to have children, which is called "sterile." No one ever dies at our parties. But just in case, I always stop at 49, so she never comes to kill anyone if I'm there. Hopefully no one is sterile, but I guess we won't know that until the future.

4. Light as a feather. One girl lies on the floor, facing up. Supine! All the other girls kneel around her, the leader at the head. Of course it's dark. Then the leader says in a spooky-whisper voice, "light as a feather," and everyone repeats it, then, "stiff as a board," and again, everyone repeats. You have to be very serious. Your hands are all around the girl, but you're only allowed to put two fingers under her, not your whole hand. There's no set number of times like 50 for Bloody Mary, so the leader has to know when everyone's about to get bored and quit. If she gets it right, then it's like everyone's in a trance, and she goes "lift," and everyone stands up and lifts. Like magic, the girl floats right up. It's really good if you choose a girl in a long white nightgown because it will look spooky. I don't know how it works. It really is magic, unless of course it doesn't work at all, and everyone is struggling and stepping on their own nightgowns trying to lift up the stiff girl, and laughing.

5. Rate calls can be fun for slumber parties, but I think they're better with only one other friend, because anything private about people who love each other can make people get their feelings hurt. Unfortunately, if you're a girl, you'll learn about gossip the hard way, how it spreads no matter what. It's just life.

6. Ice. This one is stupid. Get someone's bra, wait till she goes to sleep, put it in a bowl of water and put the bowl in the freezer. In the morning, their bra will be in a block of ice. Say you don't know who did it. Maybe it was Bloody Mary.

7. Pee. This is stupid too. Wait for someone to fall asleep, then dip their wrist in a bowl of warm water, and supposedly it will make her pee in her sleep. It never works. Sometimes Judy will talk in her sleep, but you don't need any warm water. It's always something weird and funny when someone talks in their sleep. Chris talks in his sleep sometimes and he sleepwalks too, which I hate, because sometimes he goes up to the third floor or down to the basement, and he doesn't even turn the lights on! And you're never supposed to wake someone up if they're sleepwalking, although I don't know why not.

8. One more thing: Camille has older brothers and sisters, so she knows a lot of teenager stuff, and she says when you're a teenager, you might go pool hopping. You're supposed to throw something in the pool, like lounge chairs, to annoy the lifeguards in the morning, and you're supposed to be naked. I don't know why anyone would ever do that. Also, boys and girls usually go pool hopping together. They all drive from one country club to another in the middle of the night and climb over the fence. I don't know if they're allowed to put their clothes on or a towel or what, when they get back in their cars. I am definitely not going pool hopping ever. Except I reserve the right to change my mind just in case the teenage me might think it's fun, or maybe the rules will change and you don't have to be naked.

50. Cow Tipping

Another thing some teenagers do is cow tipping. I'll be 13 soon, which of course will make me a teenager, but I can say now I will never go cow tipping at any age because it's mean. You know cows sleep standing up? If you just give a gentle nudge – or maybe a firm nudge – on their side, they supposedly rock and tip over. Some people think it's funny that cows are so stupid to just fall over like that, but farmers don't think it's funny, and I bet neither do the cows. They can even die. I would never do it and never be friends with anyone who does. Cows are nice! Their tongues are big and thick and feel like sandpaper, and they have very gentle eyes. When they look at you, it's like they always want good things for you.

51. Hanging the Rope Ladder

I was eight and Chris was six when a long-haired teenage boy stole Chris' rope ladder out of the tree by my parents' bedroom window. They heard him yell to the getaway car, and they looked out the window and watched him drop to the ground and they memorized the car's license plate, a big dark green car. Then they drove around the neighborhood and found the car and told the police they knew where the getaway car was. Then they made the teenage boy come back to our house and hang it back up, because it's Chris' rope ladder, and chopping it down is stealing. My mom sent Chris and me out there to watch him hang it back up and ask him as many questions as we wanted about why he would climb up there and steal it, was it to impress his friends that he was a tough guy, and didn't it hurt when he sawed the rope off at the top and fell to the ground, and wasn't he worried he might break his leg. He had long hair, not in a ponytail, and he didn't talk very much. Our mom said he was ashamed of what he did, and meeting us and answering our questions was punishment enough, so they didn't press charges and send him to jail.

I don't know if it really was punishment enough since he didn't really answer our questions, and I felt bad for Chris because the rope ladder used to have thick worn out beige-gray rope like from a pirate ship, and the bad guy had to buy new rope to hang it since he had cut the old rope, and that new rope was bright green, slippery braided plastic rope that you buy in a hardware store and that hurts your hands. It didn't seem like a pirate ship rope ladder anymore, which especially ruined it. I don't remember if I said what I thought of that green rope to the guy, since we were mostly asking questions instead of saying things, but I hope I told him what I thought.

I don't like the way my feet swing away, under my body when I take a step up that rope ladder. It wasn't stable even when it was pirate rope, and it didn't go up to anything anyway. My dad sometimes says we'll build a tree house, but I know we won't. It takes a lot of time and planning to build a tree house, and if he meant it, we'd see him drawing on graph paper with his T-square. I'd love to have a tree house where I could go read books and have a secret club, but it's OK not to have one because our dad has other priorities and not every kid gets to ride in boxes on a conveyor belt and push a pallet jack and earn money while they're having fun.

Buying that ugly green rope probably cost that long-haired bad guy more than he bargained for.

52. Signature Cocktails

The rope ladder was a present from Uncle Frank and Aunt Lula, and we aren't supposed to tell them about the bad guy and the green rope.

Aunt Lula says gift-giving is an art. She has a lot of arts. She says a lady needs to keep certain recipes secret, or all her recipes, because then people want to come to your dinner parties. My mom doesn't like to cook. She says your dinner party should have beautiful plates and flowers and candles and wine glasses, and the right people on the chairs, so no one cares about the food.

Aunt Lula also says you should have a signature cocktail. Signature like only you would sign your checks or your autograph if you were a movie star because then everyone would know it was really you. Everyone would know if they wanted your really special signature cocktail, like say a gin martini with an olive and a twist, and they've only ever had it like that at your house, they would know they have to go to your house to get another one, because that's your signature, and only you can do it that exact way. I don't actually know what my Aunt Lula's signature cocktail is. I think it probably has an umbrella and it's probably blue.

If she ever gives out her recipes, there's one I really want. She makes fudge and divinity every Christmas and mails us a cigar box full – one layer of fudge and then waxed paper and then a layer of divinity with walnuts. I like the divinity best, but the fudge is good too. My mom says they both have empty calories which is why people get so fat at Christmas.

53. Chicken Pox

Last year I got the chicken pox from my brother who got it from Maggie Hardmann. My case was the worst and my timing was the worst because I had it for Spring Break. They were in my ears and on my eyelids and on my tongue near the back of my throat. After it was over, and I was back at school (I didn't miss one day of school), everyone asked me how did I scratch my tongue near the back of my throat, and it's just what you think it is, you move your tongue back and forth on the roof of your mouth even though it doesn't really help. I had to stay inside and wear my purple flowered nightgown every day and Calamine lotion and white cotton Easter gloves so I wouldn't scratch. My brother played outside without me and I wasn't allowed to be jealous and our mom wouldn't make him stay in because it wasn't his fault he'd already had it and now his were gone. There was no reason to keep him in when I was the one who was sick.

The worst one was on my arm. I couldn't stop scratching it, even in my sleep, even when I wore the gloves. That one left a scar. A little dot right there on my arm. Since I missed the whole Spring Break, our parents said we could have a special summer and go to camp in Colorado with horses and hiking and mountains for a whole month. Chris came to camp too even though he got his whole Spring Break. But camp was so fun. There were kids there from Mexico and Iran and Puerto Rico and France, and I am going to stay friends with all of them, even though it's kind of hard to write letters with the language barriers. In Iran the alphabet isn't even the same as ours, but I'm still going to try to stay friends with those kids. Hopefully if I send letters, they will find someone to translate, and write me back in English. If they write me back in Persian, I'll have to try to find a translator here, and that might be a challenge. It's funny how much easier it is to speak to someone in person than it is in letters through different languages, even if you have a translator. My friend Carlos spoke almost perfect English in person – enough that I could understand almost perfectly by the end of camp anyway – but when he sends me letters, the English is really perfect, but it's his teacher who writes the letters for him and so his handwriting looks like an old lady being very careful, and it's not like him at all. It makes me miss him even more than if he didn't send me the letter in the first place. That's the trouble with translation and other people's handwriting getting in the middle of when you're just trying to say something between friends. Even if you don't have the same language, and you don't know the exact right word to use, I think it's best to talk right to your friend, in person or a letter, in your own handwriting with your own mistakes, because at least that way, it really comes from you. Anyway, you can tell a lot by a cheerful green marker and if you draw some butterflies in the margin, or sometimes I like to draw a tree with lots of leaves weaving up the page and flowers near the roots where I'll sign my name, "Love always, your friend, Sandy." I think communication with your friends is probably about expressing your intentions more than anything. And all I really want to say to Carlos is I miss him and his brother Jorge, and I hope life's good for them.

Mom and Dad said if I want to go to both sessions this year I can, but I have to pay for the second session myself. I think I'm going to earn the money though because I'm already halfway there and we don't have to pay the camp until March. Luckily there are lots of children in our neighborhood who like me as their babysitter.

54. The F-Word

In my family we don't say bad words. Not even the f-word which is fart. If someone accidentally does it, we normally wouldn't comment because that's rude. People who talk about it aren't allowed to come to our house. If they accidentally do it, that's OK though, even if they laugh, because people sometimes laugh when they're embarrassed, and no one can always control what their body does.

Snot's rude too – to talk about it and to pick it out with your fingernail. If we ever saw a person eat it, they would never be our friend again, especially if they have nice dresses and bad manners. Our mom couldn't have that. We don't call it snot, we call it gunk. In New York, your gunk is black. Here it's light green or almost white. Mom says the whole world's gunk is light green and this is how it should be, but she still doesn't like living anywhere except New York.

Also, she has noticed people here say warsh, like "I use a warsh cloth to clean my face." They don't spell it with an r, wash cloth, but it's there in the word when they say it. She says we shouldn't trust people who say warsh.

55. The Biggest Question

The biggest question we all know – in my family anyway – is when the bank will call the loan. When you build a business with your bootstraps, you don't always imagine there's a loan involved, but if you borrow money from your rich dad, that's still a loan. Although that kind of loan doesn't come with the same worries as a bank loan, when the bank can call the loan. The thing is, you have to start with money because you have to spend money to make money. There are expenses, you know, overhead, like lights and air-conditioning, actually over your head or in the wall, and there are taxes and fixing the iron railing on the shipping dock steps when a truck backs into it and mangles the railings, and so you have to have some money to start.

We have 1,200 member stores, which you write with numbers, but when you say it, you say "twelve-hundred member stores," most of them not starting with Q. Most of them pay their bills on time, but some don't. Some of the stores are suffering. My parents used to say "struggling," but now they say "suffering," so I guess things are getting worse for people. Some of the stores already went out of business, so it's probably more like "eleven-hundred-sixty-five member stores."

The Quilting Bee in Des Moines is the only one I can think of that starts with Q. I know most of the stores because I fold and stuff the invoices in the summer when I'm here.

Last summer I didn't work for four weeks because I was at camp. And this summer coming up I won't work for five weeks. I earned all the money to send myself to camp for both sessions, like I planned, but then my camp sent us a letter that they closed down. I was really sad. Really, really sad. I have a lot of camp friends I wanted to see again. But then my mom came up with an idea that now I'm pretty happy about. I made enough money to buy my airplane ticket to Saipan. Joy moved there because of her dad's job, and we write letters every month – sometimes more. She sent me a picture, and her hair is white now from living on an island. I can't wait to see her. She swims in the ocean and the pool every single day. The ocean water there is almost the same color as the pool. I think Saipan is going to be the most beautiful place in the world I will ever visit, and I plan to go to a lot of places! I'm not scared to fly by myself. It's not like a bus or a train. They won't let you get on the wrong plane.

56. Screamroller

The biggest question in my family, and probably in any business, is how long you can keep it up if there's a bank loan hanging over your head, and at any minute they might call the loan. But I had a big personal question I had to actually answer, not just think and talk and worry about like grown-ups do. I've noticed that really big questions are sometimes about how long a thing is going to last or when something big is finally going to happen.

I was in 5th grade, when I was eleven. I don't really know if that's early or late or normal or not. I think I told you my dad supposedly went on his first date at age nine. That's the trouble with the word normal – it's probably impossible to pin it down. You never know if you're only comparing to a small group of people who happen to live in your town or your neighborhood or be closest to you, and so you think "oh great, I'm normal" or you might think the opposite "oh no, I'm not normal," but in a different place with different friends, you might be completely normal. You might even be popular.

That's probably a good thing to remember. You have to do what you think is best, deep down, and hopefully you'll find your friends who make you feel normal. You might even have to move pretty far away to find them, maybe even to a foreign country. Singapore. Or Sweden or Switzerland or Spain or Saipan. Moving would be hard, but soon enough you'd realize you're at home there, so it's worth it.

Anyway, the first question in line for the Screamroller was who would sit with who because it was me and Page and Todd Barnes and Jamie Gold, and I kind of knew that Todd liked Page, and it was starting to seem like she liked him back. It was our first night trip to Worlds of Fun without parents, instead of hot sun and melting popsicles and black asphalt in the daytime and strollers and sticky little kids running around. Normally for a night trip to Worlds of Fun, somebody's parents would be eating funnel cakes and waiting for us at a table near an overhead lamp with a lot of moths, but this time they dropped us off at the entrance. Page arranged it all with her mom. So I said OK, I'd ride the Screamroller with Jamie, and Page could ride with Todd, and everyone seemed happy.

Then they asked what would happen if when we all put our arms in the air and screamed going down as always, (even though I am not a screamer and I don't put my arms up), what if when we lowered our arms, Jamie's arm might come down on my shoulder – what would happen then? That's always the question with everything dangerous. What would happen then? Todd's arm might come down on Page's shoulder. Todd and Page both seemed to like this idea, with all their nodding and smiling, and so now the big question was mine.

I think a lot of times a girl has a boy put his arm around her without asking. Like in a movie where the boy yawns and then accidentally-on-purpose puts his arm around the girl who has to pretend she's just watching TV and doesn't notice, or if it's a totally different kind of movie, (or she's a different kind of girl), when he puts his arm around her, she might kiss him like she's been waiting all her life for this chance. But I love someone else, and I didn't really want Jamie's arm around me, or I never did before that question anyway. But I was glad at least he asked so I could think about it rather than pretending it was an accident and just doing it. I would never fall in love with a boy who's a faker. And it's not like you can yawn and pretend on the Screamroller.

The line was really long, the way it snaked back and forth and back and forth, everyone ambling forward between those fake wooden fence rails, smooth and shiny from so many hands, as people move along thinking about their decisions or thinking about nothing at all. But now the question was all mine, the question, was I willing? That was the phrase they said I had to say when I decided. It sounded like a formal contract, something legal, if I said it. As we got to the front of the line, I hadn't really made a decision, I just suddenly figured what the heck. It seemed like it would make everybody happy, and it wasn't a big sacrifice for me, so I said, "OK, I'm willing."

Afterwards I sort of wished I hadn't even though it was no big deal. It's just you can't ever get that back – the first time a boy puts his arm around you, on a rollercoaster or wherever you are, and I might have done it different had I thought it out a little more. On the other hand, it could have been some faker with a stupid yawn who got me first, so now I know I will grow up with a good feeling about Jamie Gold because he was brave and asked.

57. The Boy I Love

I keep this mostly to myself, but I know if you write a book, you have to be brave enough to put the truth in it, so I'm going to tell you. I've told Lizzie, of course, and I've told Joy. I told Barbie too, even though she's not my best-best friend, but one time, she shared something extremely personal with me, and I wanted to reciprocate so she wouldn't regret trusting me. I trust her and wanted to be sure she knows I do. It's funny how you can trust certain friends you don't even know that well, whereas you don't always totally trust your best friends.

Anyway, probably everybody kind of knows because it's the kind of thing they figure out. Before I ever said it to anyone though, I said it out loud in Aunt Lula and Uncle Frank's camper when no one was there, because if you can say a secret thing out loud, then you give it to the universe for all times and make it true. The boy I love is John.

I believe in true love because I loved him the minute I met him and I've never stopped, even when he's not doing anything smart or funny or nice or anything, and even when he's absent. You can't explain it. If he falls in love with someone else, I will still love him of course, but then it will just be a fact, without a hope for the future. I guess depending on who it is, I would be pretty jealous. I would love him even if he didn't love me back, but deep down I think he does. It's just a feeling. But also, sometimes you get proof of a thing you want to know. Some people still won't believe you though, which might hurt your feelings because you told them something personal and they rejected it, which feels like they rejected you, so you ought to not tell them even if you want to. That's just life.

I had a dream one time that we both went to drink from the drinking fountain at the same time. I was holding the button to shoot the water out and he was there drinking next to me in the dream and our cheeks were touching. It was the best dream ever and how I know he loves me. You get the truth in mysterious ways. And also, his dad was being silly at my parents' dinner party and he told me too.

58. Leiben

My parents said, "We need to prepare you. Your grandma won't be like herself, with the cancer, with the stroke. She's lost a lot of weight. A stroke does funny things to a person's brain."

And I said, "Well, maybe she'll be OK, like a miracle, she'll still be OK." But I also told them I would prepare myself because that was obviously what they wanted me to say, even though I don't actually know what it means, how a person prepares herself.

And they said I had to keep an eye on Chris because he has a hard time with hard things. So I promised to do that too, without knowing what that meant either.

We went in the room at the hospital where my uncle works (she was very fortunate to have a doctor for a son, everyone should plan this if they can get a doctor for a son, even though he's not a cancer doctor and not a stroke doctor, it's still good to be in a hospital where your son works when everyone thinks you're dying). The room had kind of a skinny corridor so I couldn't see in at first because my parents went first, but then we got all the way in, my brother and me, and my parents, and my parents were right. It didn't look much like my grandmother in that bed. She didn't look like herself or like anyone ever because she had no hair and she had no teeth because they were on the table and she had no legs, or so it seemed, because she was so skinny they had disappeared under that mustard-colored blanket. It was a loose-weave blanket that your fingers get caught in when you sleep. Whether or not it was my grandmother there without teeth, I felt bad about that, that any person would have one of those blankets that catch your fingers when you're already in the hospital probably having a pretty bad time as it is.

But her eyes were sort of still her eyes, her blue eyes, and she said a word, a sound or something with that tongue in her skinny mouth, like she was chewing on her tongue, and while she chewed on that word, it seemed that with her mouth and her eyes, it seemed as though she smiled. She got stuck on just that word she started saying right when she saw my brother and me. *Leiben*, my mother told us later. I don't know how to spell it, but that's what it sounded like. It's Yiddish. It means love. It seemed like a very nice word to get stuck.

59. Rosalee Trotter Works Reception

Rosalee Trotter isn't the receptionist we had last summer. Rosalee wears long, full skirts, long hair, and glasses. Last summer we had Crystal, who taught me how to be a receptionist and wore denim cut-offs and halter tops, which is inappropriate at the reception desk even if you're as flat-chested as a boy. Crystal's other job was working on the highway, and no one told her you can't dress in an office the way you do on the highway. We have Amish families sometimes come buy fabric, and they shouldn't have to see Crystal's skin all on show. I asked my dad why no one told her to wear a dress with a lace collar or at least sleeves, and he said she wasn't staying. That seemed like a bad reason, because maybe if she could dress the right way, she could stay, and she might like working in an air-conditioned office more than the highway with the big machine that smells like tar. But anyway, she's gone now. I liked her. Luckily, I like Rosalee too.

We have a buzzer to let people in, if we see them through the window and they look OK. Sometimes a weird or scary person will come in the main door, and we have to pretend the buzzer doesn't work till they go away. And if they don't go away, we have to go get help, maybe from Dick Ferguson who talks so loud on the phone I can hear him in the front office from two rooms away. I always use the intercom to call him, "Dick Ferguson line one please, Dick Ferguson line one," and he yells over everybody's heads "Who is it?" When he answers the phone he just shouts his last name into the phone. "Ferguson!" If I was a customer, I'd be afraid of him. But hopefully if a bad guy ever comes to the door, and I have to call Dick Ferguson, the bad guy will also be afraid.

I never want to go get help because it's only a big glass window there, and if I have to come around the reception desk to get help, the bad guy would see me, my whole body in my dress, not just my head and shoulders and telephone and adding machine at the desk, and he could shoot me through the window. Mostly though, my dad says anyone who shouldn't come in would be harmless – maybe only lost. For some reason people get lost a lot around here. I guess there's someone I don't buzz in about twice a week, which I would say is a lot. Sometimes they yell through the glass they want an application, and I have to say we aren't hiring which makes me feel bad because they can see I'm pretty much just a child and what kind of company can hire a child and not a grown man who might be lost and needs a bath, but at least he's trying to get a job?

I get a lot of paper cuts, slipping invoice papers into the alphabetizer file. You might think you need two alphabetizers, one for the whole alphabet, and another one when you do each letter, but you don't. The company has a second alphabetizer file, but someone might need the other one in another department. At reception, you take all the invoices out, one letter at a time, and make criss-cross stacks with them on your desk, and then your alphabetizer is empty and ready to alphabetize the A's and then the B's and so on. You have to fold the paper right to make the address show through the window when you stuff the envelope, and you add the statement stuffer behind the invoice so the address still shows.

An invoice is the first paper a customer gets telling them what to pay. A statement is the same thing, only it's like a recap maybe even showing money they owe on a couple invoices back. You can't let it go on too long, or they will take advantage. At some point you will have to freeze their account and not let them buy any more until they pay. Even if you give a customer 30 days to pay, they might miss their deadline, sometimes by accident, and sometimes on purpose, and you have to keep track of it all. Most people intend to pay for what they buy, but times are tough and people have to feed their families. But also, you have a business to run. You have to be firm but fair.

The statement stuffer tells people about "opportunity buys" so they can save more money if they happen to need that thing at that time, or if they guess right that they will need it soon. That's a big secret of good business – timing. Our member stores are mom-and-pop shops who carry what we sell to them. "Carry" is another word for sell. Well, they hope to sell it, I mean. They stock it. That is, they keep it on their shelves, and if someone buys it, they will get another one for the shelf so it's there for the next customer. Shelf space is expensive, so they have to choose carefully what to carry. There's a lot to figure out, if you don't want to go out of business before you can pass your mom-and-pop shop down to your children.

Our business helps them compete with big huge stores in big towns that a lot of people are starting to go to, even though you might have to drive pretty far. The big stores charge less because they buy things in bulk and in China. So our member stores can buy only what they need from us, because we are the ones who buy stuff in bulk. But we mostly get everything from American companies so it's still not that cheap. You are always going to lose customers to stores with lower prices, even if the customers are your old friends and neighbors. That's just life, unfortunately. And as my mom says, life isn't fair. It doesn't mean you should stop doing a good job though.

My dad has the deepest voice on the intercom. No one wants to get called into his office, including me. Kind of like the principal. We all have to do what's good for business so the bank won't call the loan. Until last summer, all my brother and I could do was staple papers and stuff envelopes and shake people's hands at trade shows, but now I can answer phones, and when appropriate, buzz the door.

Last summer we worked half the summer and then went to camp for four weeks. This summer when I go to Saipan to stay with Joy, I'll go for five weeks, and it will be my first adventure overseas. I've been up to Canada with my family and down to Tijuana, Mexico, which are both out of the United States but you don't actually go overseas to get there. You just go in the car. I am saving Italy for the future so I can remember my grandmother in Rome. It won't be the same as going with her like we planned, but I will have her with me in spirit. I know when I go, if I ask the Trevi Fountain about a wish, I will get an answer, and it will be the truth. Not everyone in Rome is Catholic, but most people are. The Pope lives there, so it makes sense. In case you didn't know, the Pope's Catholic.

The weird thing now is I don't miss my grandma, but I think about her lots. I don't know if there's a word for that. I'm not sad. My mom is sad, she misses her the way you're supposed to miss someone you love, with sadness and soft worn-out love that lies on your couch and if you try to fold it up and lay it neatly on the arm of the couch, you come back and it's always there again waiting for you on the cushions, wrinkled up. I'm not sad like a hand-knitted Afghan like that. For me, it all stays neat and ironed, not even on the couch but on my shoulders, and I don't always notice it even when it's there, but when I want to, if I'm feeling chilly, I can shrug it close like a, well, like a shrug. That's a little jacket, you know, that you close with frogs. High fashion ladies like my grandma and my mom all know about frogs and shrugs and white fur muffs.

You need to bring your passport when you go to Saipan. The best thing of all (besides seeing Joy and going boating and swimming and hiking in the forest where the Japanese soldiers were and the forest where the American soldiers were) is they speak a different language there: Chamorro. Also, they chew betelnuts. I sort of want to try that, if it's not bad for you. People there learn about betelnuts from their parents and grandparents, but just because something's normal in a whole culture doesn't mean it's OK. So I don't know yet if I will chew any. It's OK to just say "no, thanks, I'm good." Add that last phrase so they know you're confident.

But here's what I learned this week from Rosalee. She drinks water from a mason jar she refills from the drinking fountain ten times a day if she remembers, because last year she had a urinary tract infection, and she said it really hurts and she never wants another one. You have to drink a lot of water and flush your system out like plumbing. Once you get one infection, it's easy to get another one. The word for that is "susceptible." Diseases and other bad things work like that, like with bad friends and bad grades, and bad things that get you in trouble with your parents... It's smart to avoid getting the first one. Like with smoking. You should never start because once you do, it's hard to quit.

Rosalee's sister works in domestics, and we helped her hang a beach towel display in reception. "Domestics" means sheets, towels, and stuff for your house, because the word "domestic" comes from house in Latin. *Domus.* On the phone sometimes people ask what we sell and the answer is: menswear, womenswear, sewing notions, fabrics, domestics, and shoes. Pretty much everything they need in a mom-and-pop shop except groceries.

At 11:45 the Mobilteria comes and honks its horn, and it's the receptionist's job to say into the intercom "the Mobilteria's here." You only say it once, and the warehouse guys come out to buy a sandwich. They use the front door to go out, and they say hello to the receptionist when they do, but they go back in through the shipping dock, so you're only going to say hi to them the one time. Last summer Crystal told me we can say "the roach coach is here," but never on the intercom.

60. Thunderstorm

We were all at the dinner table and it was thundering. Barley lay in the corner on the brick linoleum, watching us, like he thought we were responsible for all the noise. Like if he gave us the dog-eye enough, we'd make it stop. I don't think Barley liked it, but I like thunder sometimes. Lightning too. Not too loud, not if I'm stuck outside of course, but I love leaning over a bed, you know, propped up on my elbows with Chris or a friend, to an open window, your forehead pressed up against the screen and it's cool and humid out there and the air feels like it crackles and the rumbling is far away but still bold and forceful way off wherever it is, and you can almost hear it roll in waves like the ocean, and it makes you want to go swimming, in that gray and purple sky. And the lightning too, the way it lights up everything you've been thinking, and everything you want to see out there.

The thunder wasn't booming, it was still just rumbling far away, and no one was talking at all. Dad brings home a bucket of chicken when Mom doesn't want to cook.

We had fried chicken on our plates. I like the drumsticks best. Dark meat. My mom has not been cooking much lately. Since Grandma died, the only thing she's been making is Spaghettios or mac and cheese or peanut butter and jelly. Chris and I like all of the above, so I'm not complaining. Dad was, though. Anyway, I like chicken too.

Kentucky Fried Chicken is my favorite, except their

mashed potatoes taste like whipped plastic. You know how people say "well, you have to take the bad with the good"? No, you don't. Not always. Just don't eat your mashed potatoes. Anyway, I like the chicken, and their green beans and coleslaw. But the silence at our dinner table wasn't very nice. It wasn't the kind of silence where everyone is tired in a good way, after going for a hike or a bike ride to the park or something and we were all happy thinking about what we saw on the ride. It was just the kind of silence where everyone has too much on their minds to say anything at all to one another.

Lightning flashed outside, and I counted to eight before the thunder came. More than a mile away. A nice long rumble, and then just the gentle sound of rain.

I didn't know what else to say, so I finally said, "You guys know how I'm writing this book? It's a book about life. Do you have any advice for me to put in it?"

They all looked at me surprised, like they'd forgotten who I was, or they didn't understand what I was asking them, but at least they'd all looked up from their plates.

That's a good thing about being a writer – you can always ask a question about your book. You can always ask people for input and have something to talk about. Something fun, or just something, period.

My dad cleared his throat. "Guide to life, huh?"

"Plus some little stories," I said, "that might also help a person kind of know how to live their life." The lightning flashed again, and then the thunder – right way, but not a loud crack of it. Just some quiet drums, like when the orchestra drums are only warming up.

"Why now?" he asked.

"What do you mean?"

"You suddenly got life all figured out?" He took a huge bite off his chicken breast, and the shred of meat hung out of his mouth. Chicken grease slicked down his chin and his shiny lips. I don't think he knew. He had to sort of chomp at the meat to get it all in his mouth.

I saw my mom's fingers stretch tight on the table as she watched my dad chew.

"Just about," I said. I looked my dad in the eye. "No one can figure it out totally, but yeah, maybe. Enough anyway."

Mom said, "Why now is because her mailbox is full. Her Miss Piggy mailbox is full, the box Jessamyn Hart made for her birthday and she keeps on her dresser. All the stories she types up on Saturdays go in the Miss Piggy mailbox, and now it's full, so it's time to do the book. Right?"

I nodded. The only thing I wanted to change is that she'd said "do the book." I wanted her to say "write the book." But that was all. I lowered my hand to my lap and wiped my greasy fingers and thumb on my napkin. I didn't know she remembered that my Miss Piggy mailbox came from Jessamyn Hart.

Chris said, "I already gave you my advice for your book."

I said, "I know, it was good advice."

Mom said, "What was your advice, honey?"

"It was about bullies."

My dad said, "Ah, good," nodding, like to encourage Chris that he participated, even before he knew what Chris' advice was.

Suddenly my mom put both hands flat on the table, and she said, "Beware of strivers."

"What?"

"Beware of strivers. Beware of women striving…" It thundered, and everybody looked out the window for just a second, including Barley. Lightning comes first, if you're paying attention, but I hadn't noticed the lightning. We waited for another flash of lightning, but it didn't come and didn't come. It felt like the air was crackling in the kitchen same as outside, and it stayed quiet. I smelled the sticky mashed potatoes that I didn't want to eat.

Mom finally said, "Beware of striving women, desperate to be taken more seriously."

"And men," my dad added.

"Something going on at the office I should know?" My mom asked.

"No. Something going on in the Art Department I should know?" my dad asked. "Or the PTA or your Intellectual Women's Group?"

"Just put it this way, Sandy, beware of women who think they need to be taken more seriously than they believe they are being taken, because they're the most cut-throat people you will encounter. They will drain away your happiness and energy even as they pretend to be your friend. As soon as you can tell a woman has a point she wants to prove to you, and she wants to make you small to prove it, beware."

"OK," I said.

"You understand the phrase 'one-up-manship'?" She ate a small forkful of coleslaw and swallowed it whole.

"I think so."

She held up one finger. "Especially when you're already in a vulnerable position."

Finally the lightning flickered again outside.

We all watched her and waited for the thunder and waited for her to say more, but she didn't, and the thunder didn't come, or if did, it was very far away.

"I can put that in my book," I finally said. "I'll find a place for it."

"Good," she said. It felt like she thought she had given me the biggest clue to life on this planet for all times, but somehow I could tell it was really just a little thing, particularly for her, not for the whole world, but for her, just for now.

But still I said, "Thank you."

61. The Meaning of Life

I went to buy suntan lotion at the gift shop even though they charge a lot of money because it's a hotel gift shop, and I was running out of money with two weeks still to go on Saipan, but I already did run out of suntan lotion. You shouldn't run out of suntan lotion on a tropical island, or you'll get burned.

Normally if I was just hanging out somewhere, waiting for Joy to finish with swim team or something, it would be at the pool or the snack bar or at the beach hut or maybe down by the Hobie Cats where the Philippino men ask you to marry them. But this time I was waiting for Joy by the gift shop, and I was all alone. It was late afternoon and the sun wasn't even very strong so I probably should have saved my money and not bought new suntan lotion from the gift shop. Also, you can tell by the dust on the plastic bottles, they have them in there a long time, and I bet suntan lotion might even go bad. So it was pretty dumb to buy it there. But whatever made me do it, I went ahead and bought the suntan lotion then and there.

Actually, I do know why I went there. It was the puka shell necklaces. I wanted to go see them and decide if I wanted to buy one for Chris or even myself for when I went back home at the end of summer. They were even more expensive than the suntan lotion, so I decided I would buy Chris a t-shirt or bring him back some empty beer cans for his collection, which sounds silly, but it's something he would actually like.

A present should be what the person would actually like, even if not everybody would understand why they like it. Most everybody knows Chris collects interesting beer cans.

I was sitting at a round white metal table where you could have a drink with a blue umbrella or pull out your postcards and gift shop items from your little bag and look at what you bought. The sun was going down and you could smell hibiscus flowers and maybe lemons and chlorine and coconut that was probably someone's lotion or their shampoo, but probably not a real coconut, because they don't give off a smell like that unless they're cracked open. And even though they're everywhere on an island, they usually aren't cracked open. Maybe someone spilled something that smelled like coconut and then they left, because no one else was there.

I could hear frogs. The biggest frogs come out when it's getting dark, and sometimes they fall in the pool and drown in pool chemicals before the swim team gets there first thing in the morning. People say frogs make a *ribbit* sound, but it's really just like grunting. Almost barking. Those frogs on Saipan are big as footballs.

Beyond the hotel, the sun was going down, and even though I couldn't see it, I knew over the water the sky would be just turning pink and peach and yellow the way it does. I knew it was happening and I knew it was there like that because of the frogs and the way the air around me felt pink and pewter and a little bit purple, even, like lilac, and like if you look just from the side of your eye, not straight on, at the huge heart-shaped waxy leaves, there will be a hummingbird there in the greenery, and orange lilies to make a hummingbird feel at home, with their similar shape, and white butterflies every time. The sand is white and fine, and cool under your naked feet when the sun goes down, unless you want it warm, because there's a chill in the air, and then the sand is warm, and you can stand with your naked feet and your toes in the warm sand and watch the water and listen to the waves for as long as you like. And the water there is always calm and clear and very blue and has every kind of fish you can imagine, neon fish and angel fish and stripes and fins and colors like candies and cartoons and carnival rides. And everything smells like plumeria which is the best smell ever in the world of nature. It's a very good time to be sitting outside all alone. You can think a lot of thoughts, from the side of your mind and never straight on.

It was kind of scary going on the plane to Saipan by myself, but you just get on the plane scared and get over it. Someone says good-bye to you on one end, and someone will pick you up on the other end. If they don't pick you up on the other end, you ask the airline people to help you out, and you just wait in the airport and don't leave and don't trust anyone other than the airline people. Even people dressed as cops could be fake cops. Don't trust someone just because they're in a uniform. But mostly, there's no need to worry. Anyway, for me, Joy and her parents were there in Guam, right on time to take me with them on the next flight in a tiny airplane to their island.

So I was just sitting at the table by the gift shop minding my own business, and a Japanese mom and dad and little boy walked along from the beach toward their room in the hotel or the restaurant. The mom and dad were in nice clothes, and then the little boy, who was probably about three or four. He was in nice khaki shorts and navy blue sweater and little shoes. And the mom was in a skirt and had a nice neat black haircut. And the mom and dad were talking to their son in Japanese, which of course I don't understand, but it was just the same as if I did, because the words didn't matter at all. He was walking along with them, just behind them and I was watching and just suddenly thought *that's how it is.*

A mom and a dad get together and have a little boy, and he'll come along nicely just behind them, wearing the same kind of clothes that they wear, those nice little khaki shorts, and speaking the same language they do, and going away on trips that they go on, and smelling the coconuts and lemons that they do as they walk across a hotel patio with big green leaves and flowers and hummingbirds, and then it will be his turn to be the dad and find a wife to be the mom, and maybe she'll be Japanese like his own mom or maybe she'll be Indian or American or some other thing because people can choose whatever future they like and fall in love with whoever they like, and they will have a little son or daughter to walk along behind them, and the hibiscus flowers and hummingbirds, and then he or she will grow up and have a little son or daughter with a Portuguese or Irish or Iranian husband or wife and frogs and coconuts and on and on and hummingbirds and on.

And maybe they believe in God and think He's a He and you should capitalize the He, or She's a She with a capital S, or a monkey god or elephant god or there's no god but you know, like a ghost in the universe, like you can never see it, head-on, straight-on, side-view, you'll never see it but you know it's there. And maybe you believe dead people come back reincarnated, or they don't, they just die and lie there in the ground or underwater or all burned in ashes or whatever they do in their culture, maybe you believe you have to pray to your dead ancestors and they look after you from heaven and you could even make an altar or tattoo a picture of your ancestor on your arm or their name in script on your shoulder. But everyone gets to believe what they believe, even if their own parents might not believe the same thing. Like that little Japanese boy coming along in his khaki shorts might choose something a little bit different when he has a boy of his own, because he can. That's how life works.

You hear about people wanting to know the meaning of life, in cartoons and movies, and just in general, and it seemed pretty funny that there I was just a few weeks ago, not like an old philosopher hermit in a mountain cave with a beard who didn't speak for 20 years while he was figuring it out, and then he suddenly comes out of the cave and speaks, and he can speak 16 languages, and he says only one big thing that is the deepest truth he figured out... this is nothing like that at all, and I am nothing like that man at all. I'm just me, a girl with some suntan lotion that cost more than it should have, and I saw that family walking along and pretty much figured it out.

I never told anyone what I figured out though because it seemed important and special and I would never want anyone to make fun of it. If someone ever said no, that's not the meaning of life, or they said I was stupid, I would know they were wrong, but it would make me too sad. So I will never tell anyone ever, not even Joy.

Maybe the hermit with the beard figured it out right away too, but then he stays in his cave for 20 years hoping that's long enough for people to take him seriously. And also to learn all those languages.

62. Boys' Bikes Hurt Boys

Well, this is a little weird, that this page was in my Miss Piggy box, and even though I have gone through the box a hundred times, I only just found it today. I knew it was too short to be much of a story, so I guess I just wasn't reading it. I wrote this one of those first times I got to use the typewriter. I guess I was eight. Five years ago. And then I fixed it a little.

Supposedly it really hurts if you're a boy and you rack yourself, more than if you're a girl who racks herself (which I'm not even sure is the right way to use the word "rack," because maybe there has to be a penis involved), but what I want to know is who gets to decide who it hurts more? No matter who you are, obviously whoever you are, you're one or the other, so it's not like you can experience both and decide. But let's just say the scientists figured out a way to know for sure it hurts boys to rack themselves, and girls, not quite so much – then why on earth do they make boys' bikes have that cross-bar right up by their private parts, and girls' bikes have a much lower curved bar. Don't tell me that curved low bar is for girls who might be riding bikes in dresses or something, like why women in the 1800s used to ride horses side-saddle. I think Chris and I should both ride girls' bikes so no one gets racked. But he won't because that would be embarrassing for him, which seems like a shame.

One other thing. Who knows whether a dog is color blind or not? It doesn't make any sense because unless you're a talking dog who used to see colors and now you're color-blind, how could you know? And how could you tell anyone? Someday I hope we'll figure out how to read dogs' minds, but then we might not love them so much. My friend Kirsten said dogs can't see through windows, but I know that's wrong because Barley watches me if I go out and he's inside and vice-versa. Barley's very special, but he can't be the only dog in the world who sees through windows like that.

63. Big Fat Mean Feet

Scott Arthur pulls the legs off grasshoppers, which is very mean, to see them spit tobacco. He kicked me in the stomach last spring, and he got in trouble even though I didn't cry. He said it was an accident. But the accident was just that he kicked my stomach when he was aiming for my private parts, though he's not the one who told me what he was aiming for. Lizzie Hardmann told me. If he'd kicked me where he tried to, and if I'd been a boy, that would have really meant trouble. Why would God make boys' parts that stick out like that hurt so much if they get kicked? And girls' parts that are flat (and not so likely to get kicked) supposedly don't hurt half as much. Although I can't imagine how they know that.

Anyway, I'm still glad he didn't kick me there. He has big feet with those big fat tennis shoes of his. I think for the rest of my life, I'll see that shoe flying at me on the playground by the church entrance. Everyone asked me if it knocked the wind out of me, but since I could still breathe and talk afterwards, I guess it didn't.

Scott Arthur invented a recipe for fruit roll-ups and he makes his own sometimes and shares them, so he's not always mean. He hasn't done the grasshopper thing this year either. Maybe he'll grow up to be a good guy.

64. Laundry Chute

At Hannah and Bobby Kirschner's house we aren't allowed in the laundry chute. We aren't even allowed to play inside because we can't help ourselves and always end up in the laundry chute. It can hold our weight, even with clothes in there too, and even though we know more clothes might come down on us and we might get stuck and we know the washer and dryer are forbidden for good reason, we always want to hide in Hannah and Bobby Kirschner's laundry chute. So their mom makes us play outside. Sardines sometimes, and we are supposed to yell "Ollie Ollie Ockem Free" to escape but I didn't know that phrase when we came from New York, and it felt like when they taught me, I was being tricked.

Sometimes we go back to my house and all dress up like fancy ladies in the satin dresses my mom got in a trunk for ten dollars at the church bazaar. "Bazaar" is not "bizarre," although a lot of the items in the trunk are pretty weird. She found a cameo pin that was worth a hundred dollars and all those fancy clothes were worth a lot of money too, even though all she really wanted was just the trunk. My parents kept laughing when they pulled things from the trunk. Even the boys wear the dresses sometimes – a purple and a blue one – sometimes with a top hat.

65. A Hot and Scratchy Cast

Annie got a broken leg skiing in Colorado. Even though she's a gymnast and very flexible, one bad fall can do it. She said a lot of people got them and maybe if you never ski, you'd never get a broken leg. Now she has to wait and see if her leg will heal enough so she can train for the Olympics someday. I know you can get a broken leg a lot of different ways, but it's true if you don't go skiing, you won't get a broken leg from skiing. Her leg is hot and itchy in the cast, and she hates that as much as the broken leg in the first place. She has to wear her cast for three more weeks. You should never stick a metal ruler in your cast to try to scratch your leg because you might cut yourself in there and it won't heal. Nothing can heal without space around it, and air to breathe. Maybe if you think you're going to the Olympics for any sport other than skiing, you really shouldn't ski.

Annie's parents have a Winnebago, and she has slumber parties in it. My favorite is to sleep above the driver's seat, but I don't always get to, because everyone likes that spot and Annie has to pick which friend gets to sleep there.

66. Brookside on Bikes

We are normally not allowed to go to Brookside on our bikes because it's too far away, and there are busy streets and people who might not think like we do. Also there is a house on the way where something bad happened to Chris, even though I don't know the details. One time a mom on Ward Parkway told Chris it was time for him to go home, when my mom was late, and so Chris left on his own, in the dark. That family lived on a curve and a hill where people speed, and it's such a big street there aren't even sidewalks. That's where my mom found Chris, outside in the dark. My mom was livid. I don't know what she did or said to that other mom, but we all learned the word livid.

"Livid" is when you're so angry it's like every living cell in your body is flaming mad, and it's tearing all the life out of you, all that anger. If anything had happened to my brother, (which means if my brother got hit by a car and died), my mom would have killed that other bad mom ten times over and beat her to a pulp. But luckily, nothing actually happened to Chris that time except maybe he was scared – only to be honest, I don't think he really was.

Brookside is like that – like going to that boy's house with the bad mom, only no one is in charge, so you have to look after yourself in Brookside, which is probably safer than being with someone's bad mom in charge.

We were out of peanut butter, so Mom said I could go,

here take the money, and come back with the peanut butter in the bike basket. So I went and bought it and put it in my basket to bring it home. Only somewhere near that other house, that white one where something else happened, I hit a rock and crashed. I didn't get very hurt, but the basket dumped the peanut butter out on the road. The glass broke, *ker-spludge*, but mostly it seemed fine, so I brought it home, broken shards and heavy-sticky-brown in its bag inside the basket, hoping not to get in trouble. I'd already spent the money, so I couldn't say I hadn't gone for some reason, or I got lost, or they were out of peanut butter or the store was closed because it had a fire. I have a big imagination, but I couldn't come up with anything good enough. Anyway, never lie. I had four and a half blocks to figure out what to say. I rode the rest a little slow.

You can't take a risk with broken glass, so my mom threw the whole jar away, and I'm not allowed to go to Brookside on my own again. She was mad – I could tell by her breathing and her shoulders and her voice, even though she said she wasn't mad. It was probably just as well, I had no business doing her errands in the first place. The broken peanut butter was a sign, it probably saved my life from some future horrible thing she would have let me do. My dad said that to my mom, which seemed a little weird because he doesn't believe in signs. Instead of peanut butter and jelly, we had Spaghettios for dinner and no one talked.

67. Soldiers and Sailors and War

C hris and I went to stay at our uncle and aunt's house in California and we took a plane without our parents, which is called "unaccompanied minors." They got us bikes, both of us have boys' bikes here in California, with that bar that hurts you, and neither of us can touch the ground with our feet, so we have to always tip our bikes sideways when we get off and not forget. It's worth it though, to have those bikes when we're there, and really nice of them to get them for us.

There's a dirt alley behind their house, and it goes all the way down the road, behind the houses, with hardly any cars back there, just some bright green weeds sometimes and flowers and every now and then a cat. We can ride and ride down that alley. We ride around the neighborhood too, sometimes on the road and sometimes the big street with lots of cars. Aunt Lula doesn't worry unless we are gone for one hour and then we have to come back and check in. She waits in the kitchen for us and smokes. Maybe if we go there next summer, we'll be older, and she won't start to worry for two hours or more. But maybe next summer we'll go to camp. I kind of want to go to camp.

Aunt Lula puts all her hair on top of her head with bobby pins and she looks like she could be a movie star with her cigarette. She laughs a lot, she laughs at stuff we say every

time we try to make her laugh. One time she cried, and
my mom said don't make her talk about that. But that was
another time, when Uncle Frank and Aunt Lula were staying
with us. In general, we try not to talk about wars or bad guys
or anything that makes anyone cry. There are never any kids,
even at the grade school playground down the road, so we
don't have any problem coming back when our hour is up.
Maybe all the kids in California go away to camp. I don't
know, I just know there aren't any kids around except Chris
and me.

They took us camping in the mountains, by a lake where
people fish, and we slept outside under the stars so we
wouldn't get bored. Everyone should sleep under the stars
some time in their life. We went for a hike and looked out
for snakes like people do, and then we fished. I can thread
a worm onto a hook, but I have to talk to myself when I'm
doing it. *This is not gross, this is not gross, this is not gross.*
I wish the worms didn't wriggle like they do when you're
stabbing them on there.

We caught a lot of fish, rainbow trout, that only look like
a rainbow if you squint your eyes and tip them in the sun,
and use your imagination. And we made a fire and had a
cookout with our trout and then s'mores. They're very
messy! S'mores are when you roast a marshmallow over the
fire and you make a gooey sandwich with Hershey's chocolate
and two graham crackers. You have to eat it fast before the
marshmallow oozes out. When you're done, you're supposed
to say "Please Sir, can I have s'more?" Like you're an orphan
in *Oliver Twist*. I never say that though because s'mores make
me kind of sick. I might ask for some more if they didn't have
the chocolate. I love roasted marshmallows, when they're
just nice and brown! If they catch fire, you can give them
to your Uncle Frank. He likes them like that. They go great
with beer. He crunches his beer cans in his fist.

Back at their house sometimes we stayed inside and played

cards. Crazy Eights and Go Fish, mostly. Aunt Lula taught me Solitaire and how to shuffle and bridge the cards so they make a waterfall slippery paper sound. *Flip-flip-flip-flip*. I like to shuffle more than play Solitaire on the bedspread. One time I was playing Solitaire and the bed started shaking like *The Exorcist*, even though I haven't seen that movie, I heard about it, about a girl who is possessed by the devil, and her bed shakes and her head spins around like an owl – only an owl can really do that and a girl can't, even if she's possessed and the movie has special effects. Mom said the movie's silly, but maybe some religious people think it's terrifying.

I was really scared in California though, even though the bed only shook at little, but Aunt Lula asked me if I felt the tremor, which is a tiny earthquake. I was glad it wasn't a big earthquake because I did see the movie *Earthquake* with my mom and I had a lot of nightmares about that. And also, I was glad the bed was really shaking, that brown and orange flowered bedspread, and it wasn't just in my head.

Aunt Lula bought me roll-on deodorant in case I want to use it, but it's very sticky so I don't like it. I wanted the kind called Tickle, but she said it's just a marketing ploy, the way they designed the bottle and gave it a silly name that would appeal to young girls. Young girls are a big market for beauty products and things to make them smell good because we are very susceptible and insecure. Not just young girls, not just ladies, but everyone has insecurities about smelling bad and looking less than their best. Even some men worry about their looks. Everyone should beware of marketing ploys!

She told me witch hazel will clear up any blemishes and if I get a stubborn one, you can dab on toothpaste. She doesn't have any daughters so she tells these things to me. A blemish is a pimple. There are other words the teenagers will use. You'll learn them when you have them. Every generation of teenagers makes up their own words for things so they feel original when their bodies go through changes and do things that make them think they are alone, like no one in the world has had quite this problem in the world before them. They invent dances and rules and music and ways to say I love you with words and with their bodies and new words for a blemish. And I will understand all of this when I need to.

Blackhead, whitehead, clogged sebaceous gland. I told her I'd seen pictures in the science book. Aunt Lula looked at me funny. But to get rid of them, she said, the old remedies still work. Witch hazel to clean your face, after you use soap and water, and then toothpaste.

Sometimes we play War. But it takes a long time and Chris always gets bored, and me too, before anybody wins. "Is that why they call it War?" I asked her. "People get bored it if goes on too long, and they want to stop?"

She smokes Kool Menthol cigarettes, and she turned her head away with a smile on her face I could see from the side as she blew out a lot of smoke. "No, honey," she said. "That's not how war works." I guess she knows too, because my Uncle Frank was in World War Two in the Navy – he did autopsies – and my cousin's in the Army, so Aunt Lula knows about soldiers and sailors and wars.

68. Cluck

Haunted houses are supposed to be fun, but they're not. Fun houses are supposed to be fun too like that scene in *Grease* at the end when Olivia Newton-John is at the carnival in her tight black pants and lipstick and big hair, and she's dancing up and down the moving walkway thing, singing with John Travolta. The word for that up-and-down business is "undulating." But a real-life undulating walkway is not fun because if you're trying to walk somewhere, you want the path to behave itself and let you get where you're going. An undulating sidewalk is the opposite of fun, probably even if you're Olivia Newton-John. Unfun.

We went for Page's birthday party yesterday, and everyone was there: Page, Constance, Annie, not Joy because she's in Saipan – lucky Joy – Lizzie, Katherine, Judy, Barbie... all of us. Page loves Halloween because it's her birthday, so you can't blame her for always liking Halloween things, candy and costumes and scary stuff, and you can't blame her for wanting her 13th birthday party to include all 13 girls in our class. Lucky thirteen. They had to divide us into two groups – six and seven girls each. I was in the one with seven, which is sometimes my other lucky number. Not always.

I've never liked any haunted house. At Disneyland you're in a ride, and supposedly you're looking in the mirror, and the person next to you in the ride becomes a skeleton, and you're supposed to be scared, but you can still see it's your mom next to you, so that's just stupid. It's a fine line between stupid and scary, and when I'm looking for entertainment, I don't see the point in either one.

Chris screamed in the elevator the first time we went to the haunted house at Disneyland, but that's because he was little and everything was scary to him, not because the ride was actually scary. Scary things are only scary if you truly think something might go wrong, like with the ride or the people who work there, who might actually be evil.

What I can't understand is why a Haunted Hospital Room belongs in a haunted house at all, or why everyone always wants to go there. We have 15 boys in our class, and I think every single one was jealous that only the girls were going.

Haunted houses hire teenage boys who dropped out of high school and weirdo actors who have terrible ideas as to what's fun and what's funny. Then if you put a bunch of 13-year-old girls in there, those guys might go haywire, and someone will have to do something to stop it. It doesn't always have to be me. It shouldn't *ever* have to be me. But it had to be someone last night.

I couldn't very well leave Constance there on the operating table with that horrible guy with fake blood and lab coat and saw. That saw sure didn't seem like a prop. A fake one would be plastic and not so shiny. His saw was shiny. I had heard people screaming in that room before we got there, but I thought it was just actors.

The guy turned out not even to be a teenage boy either. It was a grown man with weird patchy facial hair under his doctor mask, when he pulled it off. Page's dad is going to submit a formal complaint. I hope he wasn't just saying that to calm me down. But to be honest, what happened in there wasn't the real problem. Well, it was, but now I have another problem, even realer. I know "realer" isn't a word, but your brain doesn't work so well and find the words you want when you're stressed out and mad.

The whole place was terrible, even the haunted rusty merry-go-round in the parking lot with psycho clowns and bloody dolls on the horses going up and down and round and round and round and wailing while we waited in line. One of the merry-go-round horses had a big knife stabbed right into its neck which is just cruel and unnecessary. And then of course there was the horrible undulating walkway to get in. Did I mention, I hate haunted houses?

I know I could have just screamed and squealed the whole time like everyone else like "ooh, isn't this funny..." but I could tell Constance was scared for real, and that was just from her face before I even knew she peed her pants, which her sister told me this morning when I called their house. The only reason she got away with it, the pee, was that she had her period and had a big Kotex pad in there. Very convenient. I like Sabine. Constance's sister tells the truth, and she seems to know when a person needs to hear it. Constance denied the whole thing, of course.

I know she didn't even want to go in the first place, same as me. You could tell even from what she was wearing. The same dress she had on at school all day. A pretty dress, light pink with a white ruffle and eyelet lace, but not something you'd wear to a haunted house. Definitely not something you'd want to wear into the haunted hospital room.

We had already been in four rooms, and they were all bad, but none of them were awful. I just don't like when people jump out of dark corners to startle you. Getting startled and getting scared are two different things, and they try to do both. The walls are the worst because sometimes there are people wedged in dark, tight spaces in the walls, and they grab you. So we all got into the room that said Dr. Death on the door, and the door slammed shut behind our group. Howling noises came from the ceiling. Loud banging like a hammer on metal came from below the floor, and it made my feet tingle.

The doctor guy in his bloody lab coat and face mask yelled, "Where is she? Who is my next victim?" He put his hands on his white operating table, and leaned toward us. His fingernails were black.

We all squealed and screamed and squirmed against the dark wall like of course we were expected to. It was still sort of funny. I was nervous about the wall, but no one was jumping out of it at us.

He scanned the group of us. "Who is my next patient?"

Constance jammed her head into my shoulder, and I wished I could get away from her like Lizzie had in the very first room. Lizzie's good at that if someone's bugging her. She just twists herself out of their grasp. But I guess I felt bad for Constance since she told me outside she wasn't so hot on the whole idea of the haunted house.

Something loud clanged at the far door, and I saw bars like a jail in front of the wooden door. I knew for fire hazards, you'd have to be able to get out – it couldn't be a real jail door – but it sure looked like we were locked in. Between the steel bars, you could see orange and purple graffiti sprayed on the door. It said "Dr. Death" and "Hellter Skellter" which I think was just an excuse to put the word HELL up there, but later, my dad said it was a reference to something more sinister, which means evil. It's probably the same Latin root word as *sin*. So I guess in that sense, sin's a good word to know.

Constance was grabbing my arm under my armpit, so hard it had to be making a bruise. Fog pumped from under the operating table and crept along the floor toward our feet and knees. There was a coffin under a single spotlight on the wall opposite.

"Time is running out!" Doctor Death bellowed.

Everyone crammed into a tight ball of girls, up against the wall, but it had blocks or something poking out and you couldn't get right up against it. The banging noises were still coming from the room below us. I already hated the whole place, before we'd even gotten off the haunted ferris wheel in the parking lot, but at this point it wasn't funny at all, and I was hating it pretty much ten out of ten.

Doctor Death scanned the group of us carefully. "Where is she?"

"Here!" A muffled woman's voice came from somewhere, and the coffin creaked open. "Here I am." A nurse-corpse sat up and cackled. Her hat looked like a dollop of whipped cream on a giant puff of frizzy black hair. Her eyes had gray make-up with thick, bloody tear-streaks painted down her cheeks. Her lips were black.

"Get back where you belong. You're already dead." The doctor shook his saw at her, but she climbed right out of the coffin and hopped up on his operating table, standing on it with her hands on her hips. White tights and black lace up boots and a load of sausages or hot-dogs or something meant to be guts pouring out of her stomach. She wore a really short skirt. And she was up on that table where you could pretty much look right up there. She was more disgusting than scary. The doctor jumped up and chopped off her sausages and everybody screamed and the nurse wilted like the witch melting in *The Wizard of Oz*. Then she crawled over to the coffin, dragging her cut-off sausages, and got back in. The doctor slammed the lid tight. He turned back to us, and in a flash, he was across the room and right in front of me. But it wasn't me he wanted. He reached right over my shoulder and pulled Constance away from me, which was a relief and horrible at the same time. He grabbed her by the shoulder and under the knees and hoisted her onto his operating table. He flipped four leather straps one after the next, with a loud clang each time, and had her legs and arms trapped at the edges of the table, her arms above her head, and her feet wide apart. Her naked knees looked skinny and almost blue under his operating lamp, and I was really wishing Constance had worn jeans. One of her penny loafers had fallen off and her foot looked long and bony in her white knee sock. All of us were screaming, even though Constance had gone totally still and quiet. I thought she was going to throw up. Dr. Death held up his shiny saw that had just chopped off all those sausages, and that's when I saw her face, plain as day, like she'd spoken right into my ear. "Help me." Suddenly no one was screaming or squealing any more.

"Time to play doctor," he laughed like a maniac, waving his saw around over his head. "How do we play doctor?" The loud banging kept vibrating the floor under our feet. He stuck the saw in a wide sheath at his side, stood next to Constance, and pulled on rubber gloves one finger at a time. "Come on girlies, how do we play doctor?"

No one was laughing any more. No one was moving. No one.

He reached forward with his powder-white gloved hand and started to touch the pink ruffle of her skirt.

"Stop it!" I ran forward, to try to get Constance free. "We don't play doctor, you idiot!" He grabbed both her legs, so I ran right around the table at him, swinging wild punches and yelling, "Stop it!"

There's sort of no explaining what happens when a person really wants to stop something, because it was like watching a movie, only I was in the movie, aware of it all, it was me yelling "stop it!" But I was not controlling it. Everybody started yelling, except Constance who was still there all quiet like she was dead. I'm pretty sure I punched the guy a couple times, but then I was trying to flip those leather straps to let Constance out of there, and he was trying to restrain me, so all I could do was sort of whack him with my elbows like a crazy helicopter bird swiveling side-to-side. Probably not a technique Mohammad Ali would use. And I didn't like him grabbing me one bit.

The nurse-corpse sat up and watched, laughing with her shrill cackle. I got the straps open – they actually all just flipped up once I got the one by her foot – and Constance scrambled off the table. The doctor started chasing Annie around the table until the jail door opened, and the whole time, I was still yelling. Everyone raced out, including me, and still, I couldn't stop yelling. I didn't like how he'd grabbed hold of me and pinned my elbows. Even after his hands were off me, it seemed like I could feel those awful rubber gloves and the cold fog machine pumping fog. Even now I have to force myself not to feel all that.

Page's dad came to calm me down outside. And then he had to calm Page down too, because she was so mad at me. She said it was fun – the best one ever, till I ruined it. The whole other group got kicked out without even doing the Haunted Hospital Room and they were all mad at me too. They thought the whole place was hilarious and because of me, they missed the best room. I thought Page's dad should tell them to lay off, but he didn't. My dad would have. I have a better dad than most everybody.

Apparently if a birthday group makes it through the Haunted Hospital without panicking, all the way through the human sacrifice, the birthday girl gets free entry to the Haunted Fun House the next night, and I blew that for Page. I don't think anyone should ever go back there, but I still feel bad about it, since it seems so important to Page, but it's only five dollars a ticket, and I even told her I'd give her my allowance. But then Page said I was a chicken, and everybody was laughing and saying "Sandy Sandy Cluck Cluck." Including Constance. Especially Constance. I'd like to see any one of those stupid girls on that table as scared as Constance was, and I bet they'd wish I'd do the same thing for them. I should have let Constance get human sacrificed.

I can't believe I thought she'd apologize when I called her this morning. I'm still glad I called though, because of what Sabine said. I could make fun of her about the pee so easily if I wanted! Or the Kotex pad! Who uses a Kotex pad? La

Mouse the Model didn't teach her stupid waifish daughter how it's done with periods today?

Page's dad had to go back in and get Constance's missing penny loafer, and then we all had to walk a whole block to the River Quay Zeppi's Pizza for the birthday cake. They chanted that stupid "cluck cluck" thing the whole way. When a group of people are mocking you, you have to just take it and hope it will stop on its own. You can't turn it around by pretending to laugh it off or join in. But it didn't stop the whole way to Zeppi's. My family never goes to the River Quay because it's where the mafia blows up restaurants, and there's a perfectly good, safe Zeppi's near our house. I wished I was at my own Zeppi's. I wished I was at home watching TV with Chris and Barley in my parents' bed like when we were little kids. Even something ridiculously boring like election results late into the night with our maps and lap desks and red and blue pencils. Well, to be honest, it's only me with the lap desk and colored pencils. Chris mostly just rolls around my parents' bed with Barley, pulling his lips up and stuff. I wished I was anywhere else in the whole world. Thank God it wasn't a sleepover, and I only had to wait another hour till my mom came. When they sang happy birthday to Page, I mouthed the words.

If they are still calling me Cluck Cluck at school, I don't know what I'll do. I hate the Haunted Fun house. I hate all my friends. I hate Constance and her stupid skinny foot. I should have let her get sacrificed. But then I'd hate myself. If anyone says it again at school though, I'm going to say Cluck You. I just hope she gets what I mean. When you're really fuming mad, maybe it's not smart to be so smart.

69. Bad Words

Even though my family doesn't say bad words, both my parents did, one time each. My brother was pretty sure Walt Waterstone stole his bike. He was 99-and-a-half percent sure, and also Eddie Holmes saw Walt Waterstone steal it. Eddie Holmes was 100% sure, and everyone knew those Waterstone kids were bad news, so my dad went over there – I didn't even know the Waterstones, and I didn't know my dad knew them, but he told Walt Waterstone he better come over to our house with my brother's bike in its original condition, he'd better *goddamn* bring that bike, or the police would bring that bike back and haul him off to jail. I didn't actually hear any of this, but Chris told me.

That afternoon the bike showed up with a different seat, a banana seat like on a little kid's bike, and the metal parts, the frame, had been painted black already but someone had scraped the black off so the yellow showed through again where it could. It made me sad to see that messed up black and that banana seat when it used to have a racer seat, and I wondered where the racer seat was, maybe lonely in the world, in the corner of someone's dirty garage, the Waterstones' garage, or someone else's, with old shovels and tire pumps and broken sleds. And it made me sad my dad had to use language like that, even if it served its purpose. I think it made me even sadder that it did.

My mom said *goddammit* one time. The bus was out front

for summer camp at Allendale and I couldn't find my shoes. Everyone was running around, and the bus driver was out there honking, and there were my shoes at the foot of the stairs, like they'd been waiting for me to head out the front door with all my camp stuff for the day, my riding boots and swimsuit and towel and suntan lotion, and my lunch. And there they were, my red rounded-toe tennis shoes that she calls sneakers. I think she was so happy we found them in time and so mad at me that I'd lost them that she picked them up in one hand and slammed them against her other hand like she was clapping and she yelled *goddammit*. People yell bad words when their emotions get too strong to contain.

I took the shoes with all my other stuff and ran out barefoot to the bus. I was scared at camp all day. Usually when she gets really mad, the person she's mad at is my brother. When I got home though, she said she was sorry. And the next day was the last day of camp, when parents are invited, and she won the prize for the mom who could trampoline the highest. She took pictures of me with Crackerjack, my favorite horse. The only camp prizes I won were horseback riding and shooting a twenty-two. My brother picked archery over riflery, but that's in hot sun, and it doesn't have the smells or the sounds or the lying down I like with guns. He won swimming and trampolining but not archery.

70. Socks and Undies

My brother sleeps in pajama pants. I sleep in a cotton nightgown and underpants. Lizzie and her sisters have nightgowns but they don't sleep in underpants because their parents say it's important to let your butt breathe. My mom says that's nonsense.

Sometimes we sleep in socks, sometimes not. We don't worry about socks. Brian Fullerton and his brother Justin never sleep in socks because you'll get monkey feet. I didn't even ask my mom what she thinks of that. I know she'll say that's nonsense.

I know you shouldn't rub your private parts with a soapy washcloth in the bath because it feels good now but it hurts a lot later. That's a good lesson for someone else to learn and teach you – a girl, I mean. But no one usually tells you till you learn it too late yourself, usually around age four. If I'm ever a mom with a daughter, I will have to remember to tell her about that when she's still three.

71. The Plane

Supposedly if you write about a terrible thing that happened to you or someone you love, it takes some of your pain away. You can learn that from Anne Frank, but of course Anne Frank still got put in the concentration camp and died, so if it helped her to write about being stuck in the attic of that little house, I guess that's good, it probably made her feel like she had a friend in there her same age, when she was writing in her diary, but the result of the bad thing for her was still the same. That's how you know it's true and not fiction. If *The Diary of Anne Frank* was fiction, she would have survived the Nazi invasion and she would have grown up to have a family of her own and also she probably would have saved a bunch of small children in Holland and made it into a cartoon movie with birds and singing skunks. Actually, they did make it into a movie, even though it's not a happy ending, so it's like a real movie. I think the scariest sound I've ever heard is those sirens in that movie that they have in Europe, and supposedly, they still use those sirens there today, which if I was in charge of the world, I think I would make them never use those sirens again anywhere in the world. But it's important to remember terrible things that happen so history won't repeat itself. So I guess the sirens should stay.

I was going to tell you about what happened, but even when I start to type the words, I can't breathe and I have to stop.

Dad took Barley out to that big field by the duck pond,

and no one is supposed to have their dog off-leash there but they all do, and Chris and I were throwing bread to the ducks with Mom, and no one is supposed to have remote control planes there, and no one ever does, but a man did yesterday, a man with his son who was older than Chris but younger than me, so just a boy, and it surely wasn't on purpose, my dad says it surely wasn't on purpose, but he flew his plane and it was pretty big and it hit Barley. He was running in the field. Dad had thrown the tennis ball. The plane was flying and it hit him and Dad carried him to the car and didn't even come tell us, because the car keys were in his pocket, and it was just a coincidence that he had driven to the park to meet us there because we all walked and met him there when he finished at the office, and the car was right near that field above the duck pond. It was a heavy plane, I guess, heavier than you might imagine for something that could fly, that's supposed to only be a toy, really, and Barley died. And I'm sorry but it's not making me feel any better to write this down.

I can type without seeing the keyboard. I can type this.

He was very soft. He sang when the telephone rang like it was music. He grabbed the mail when the mailman poked it through the mailbox in the front door. He didn't like cinnamon rolls but he would eat them. My dad had to carry him to the car and the vet couldn't save him. He did not suffer. That's a terrible, terrible thing to say because it's supposed to make you feel better but it still means the person died. Dad drove him straight to the vet and didn't even come back to the duck pond to tell us, and he took an hour and a half, and that man with the plane had to come and tell my mom what happened. And I saw him talking to her and I knew it was something bad, even though they stepped away to the bridge where we had our flying up ceremony for Brownies, so I couldn't hear them, but I could tell it was something bad. The man looked so serious and he kept glancing up the hill where his son was holding the plane, and I was looking up there for my dad and Barley and my mom was holding her hands together tight like if there was a bug trapped in there and it was flitting around annoying her but she had to be sure not to let it go. You can tell exactly what people are saying if you watch them. And his son waited on the other side of the pond, holding the plane. I hope it was the man and not his son who was flying the plane because I bet that boy must feel almost as bad as I do even though he didn't love Barley and didn't even know him, maybe he even feels worse. Maybe that man and his son don't know Barley died. Probably the dads exchanged phone numbers though. Grown-ups always give and take their numbers.

I don't feel any better. I don't think I will ever feel any better.

72. Bed Bugs

This isn't a story, it's just an old page I typed one time, one of the first times I got to use the electric typewriter. It doesn't even fit here for any reason, except that I can't write anything new. My brain is like an old dried-up hard kitchen sponge with nothing in it. I think I might never have anything good to write ever again.

We don't pray on our knees by the bedside like they do in books of Christmas stories. Neither do Lizzie or her sisters or Annie or any one we know. In the books the children put their prayer hands together and ask God out loud to look after them while they're sleeping so they don't die and then they list all their relatives to please not die also. I can't imagine God's that dumb He'd need a reminder not to let all those people die. And then they say "amen" and get in bed, and their parents tuck them in and say "don't let the bed bugs bite," and then the children go to sleep.

But I think bed bugs aren't real. If they are real, how could you let them bite you or not let them bite you if you're asleep? Mosquitoes always bite you when you're asleep and also, when you're awake. Mosquitoes like my brother because he is very sweet. I am not so sweet. They don't bite me as much as Chris, but they do like to go in my ears at night and make a horrible high-pitched noise that says *Iwanttolandonyou... Iwanttobiteyou... yourarmorlegorshoulder... suckyourblood... sucksucksuck... putmyteenytinypoisoninyou... suckyourblood...* Sometimes I hit my ears to make them stop. But at least I don't have bed bugs. I wish all the mosquitoes could turn into fireflies, and then I would let them suck my blood if they want because I love fireflies and I think they would light up red and blue and rainbow colors when they come get their dinner from my arms, depending on what I had for dinner. I would try to eat every colored dinner, especially blue. Though there aren't very many blue foods. Blueberries.

73. Qwerty

All I could type today was qwerty. That's what they call the keyboard because it's how the letters are arranged. So I practiced letters, but I didn't have any words to use them for.

Maybe I'll have some stories later, maybe by next week, but right now I can't even imagine that. For now my brain is still hard and crumbly, and I still don't know if it's ever going to be better. I can understand how creative people just dry up. Artists and stuff. That's exactly what it is. You just dry up, even when you tell yourself to get over it, you're not all dried up, chin up, and all that. You just stay all dried up. Mom brought Barley's bowls and bed to the Salvation Army. They said sorry for your loss and she came out to the car and cried for a long time before she could drive, while Chris and I stayed very quiet in the back. I have never felt more like crying in my whole life but I couldn't because it seemed like only one person should be allowed to cry at a time. Maybe Chris thought so too, because he didn't cry either. Also, it's kind of scary when your mom is crying and crying in the car. A person feels all dried up and empty, then there are tears, and you're sweaty and you're all wet. It doesn't make any sense.

74. In-between

Some people say there's no such thing as God or Heaven or Hell or dog heaven or angels or an afterlife or any of that, we are just bodies, we are all just animals on planet earth, with our little temporary animal families and friendships and connections, and none of those mysterious things are true, and I don't know about any of it any more than any other human being knows. But I am going to tell you one thing I know. Last night I had a dream with Barley in it. I know it came from my own brain, I know what a brain scientist would say about a dream, but let me just tell you this anyway.

He was his normal happy dog self, like he was a week ago, and he was barking and jumping around with his ears flipping up and down and inside out, but the weird thing is even though it was barking and sounded like barking, I could understand him. We were someplace small and dark, but he had a sort of light on him, right on his mouth, and he was talking. Not at first, though. At first, it was like "woof, woof," but then it was "wee, wee," only I knew it was "*oui, oui*," because it turned out in my dream, Barley could speak French. And then it wasn't dark at all anymore, but sunny, and we were outside. I bet dogs speak every language in real life. And then it was Chinese, which is weird because I'm not sure they love dogs in China like we do in America and England and Switzerland and France and everywhere, well, everywhere in the Western World. But if Barley speaks

Chinese, even if only in my dream, it just goes to show you how he gets along with everybody.

And yeah, I'm saying gets along, in the present tense, because it was that kind of dream that's like it's real. We were in a field with lots of purple flowers and yellow ones, and trees all around the edges. I'm still in a good mood from it, even though I'm totally awake now. But that's the best kind of dream, the in-between dreams that you are still asleep and dreaming, and somehow you already know it's a dream even when you're dreaming it, but the good part is still happening. I like in-between dreams and things. There's all this movement in the in-between, it's not just one thing or another thing, it's not past the last thing, and it's not fully starting the next thing, you know? Like childhood and then you start the early part of being an adult, even though you're not really there yet. It's not either/or, it's not neither/nor, because it's both! It can still be anything! It's the spaces between all your thoughts, when they're interesting and exciting and waiting patiently, and you want to choose which one to think about next, and you can choose because there's space in-between them, organized so you can see clearly. Nothing's all over-crowded on-top-of-each-other or clogged up in your brain or crammed together, competing. It shimmers and it's iridescent. I can't explain that – I can only tell you that it is. That's another thing I mean about in-between. It's the magic calm, quiet space and healthy gaps in time that let you breathe a little and think about the dream you just had and are sort of still having, or about the day you're about to have and are sort of already having. It's like when you're about to open a present, and your hand is just under the Scotch tape on the wrapping paper but you haven't torn into it yet. That's also the in-between I mean. Or say you're in fourth grade and the boy you like accepts your rate call and you haven't even said the name yet – your name – but you can just tell he's going to say eight or something good. But the split second before he says it, it's like the room is filled with invisible sparkles and music you can feel and barking that's also talking, and it's really wonderful like magic. And then he says eight and it's all true.

So I was laughing in the dream and petting Barley in the sunshine in that field, and so happy I was laughing. I think I might have been laughing in my sleep, out loud. Don't you love it when you're so happy your body does something you never meant to do like laughing? Barley's ears were all fluffy, soft and warm, and his tail was wagging so hard it was spinning him in circles just like always, and I stopped him spinning just for a second, since he could talk and it was such a great opportunity. I held his face and said, "Barley, you can talk!" He just smacked his lips, and I said, "Are you OK? Is it – I mean, you're OK! Are you OK?" He licked my face, maybe because I had tears coming out, even though I was so happy, and I probably tasted nice and salty, and he said in English, "Yup." Like a bark this time, but it was the word "yup." And then in his funny dog voice, "It's all true, Sandy Drue." Just like that.

And then he scampered off. I wanted to ask him about Grandma so I could tell my mom, and well, I wanted to ask a lot of things, but I guess I got my answer. I wanted to ask him to go see Chris in his dream because Chris has been really sad about Barley dying. We all have. People gave my mom flowers and they gave Chris a stuffed dog that looks like Barley at school, which was really nice, and Annie gave me a keychain with a dog that looks like Barley and John told me at school he was really sorry to hear about Barley, and it seemed like he might have also been crying, and even Mark Martinez didn't do up-for-grabs with his Hostess cupcake like he usually does because he loves to cause chaos, but he just put it on my desk like it was the most normal thing in the world, and everyone seemed OK with that. Those things are all really nice to know we have friends who care about us, but we have still been so sad. I had never seen my dad cry before.

When he came home from the vet and told us Barley was gone and didn't suffer, Dad had to squeeze the bony part of his nose with his fingers, and my mom jumped up and hugged him, and they stood there hugging like that for a long time. She says when we lose someone we love, they are still here with us, whenever we think of them. I like that idea, but I don't know – I didn't know – if it was true. And then look what Barley came to say in my dream.

This morning I told Chris that maybe Barley would come to his dream sometime too, and I don't know what's true or not true, or what's only in a person's brain when they're asleep or awake or what's only ever going to be a mystery no one can solve, but I know I felt better in the morning, and so that's no mystery to me. Everyone can believe what they want, anything and everything, and I can believe what I believe, and I know it's true.

75. Solved

I started writing my stories and advice and rules and things when I first came to work Saturdays and that's when I first switched schools because of the teacher's strike in 2nd grade. That's age seven to eight. I didn't actually find too much to put in from the first few years because they were mostly just recaps about hockey games, but still, it's a lot of little things I have put together here from the last few years. So the big question is how do you know when your book is over? If it's Nancy Drew, it's over when the mystery's solved. Nancy Drew is lucky to always have exactly one mystery to solve in every book. Maybe in the future I will write mysteries. With this book, I didn't even realize I had a mystery to solve, and then suddenly I think I kind of solved it. That must make my mystery a seriously mysterious mystery... which explains why I say I only kind of solved it. A seriously mysterious mystery probably can't ever be fully solved. But for me anyway, I guess I've got my answer.

Acknowledgements

This novel is for my mother and in special memory of Mattie Harris. I dedicate it also to my readers. Thank you for investing your valuable time with my words. I am honored and grateful.

My gratitude also to dear friends, supporters, early readers, and editors: Michelle Bailat-Jones, Meg Gardiner, Brian Gresko, Jose Varghese, Katie Hayoz, Daniela Norris, Susan Tiberghien, Anna Solding, Erin Salada, Jude Polotan, Tim Carl, Jacqueline Henry, Madhushree Ghosh, Sharon Van Epps, Kathi Hansen, Mary Albanese, Susie Brand, Sophie LeRouge Knight, Jackie Hayden Wilson, Margaret Fletcher Saine, Meg Brennan Hamilton, Gladys Talai, Bonnie Boyles, Kirsten McGannon, and Mary Knapp Parlange. Enormous gratitude to the Sirenland Writers Conference, specifically Dani Shapiro and Andre Dubus III. I'm also indebted to the 13th International Conference on the Short Story in Vienna, Austria – in particular to Dr. Sylvia Petter for the invitation to this remarkable gathering of so many wonderful writers doing exciting things with fiction... Sandra Jensen, Sandra Cisneros, Robert Olen Butler, Pat Jourdan, Vanessa Gebbie, Tania Hershman, Cate Kennedy, and Tom Kennedy, to name just a few. Heartfelt thanks also to my writerly lifeline in the Geneva Writers Group, Iowa Summer Writing Festival, American Women of Surrey Writers, the London Author Fair, UCLA Creative Writing, the Lavaux Literary Salon, Gobreau Press and Delphi Distribution. I am blessed beyond measure by the support of John, Jack, Edward, Ace, Tim, Heather, Ian, and Sam. In a search for the meaning of life, you're my answer.

Finally, thanks to 8th grade Creative Writing teacher Eric

Fridman, who lit the spark of this novel years ago, and to my father, who supplied paper, black and red typewriter ribbon, White-out, and regular access to his IBM Selectric with its magical golf ball.

Readers' Group Discussion Guide

No two people read a novel the same way. Personal experiences encourage new themes and ideas to emerge during discussion, enhancing each individual reader's understanding of the story. The following questions are intended to trigger conversation about *Mailbox*, its concept, tone, structure, and characters. Gobreau Press welcomes your comments online, at Goodreads or other readers' social networks. Please let us know what inspired you and your discussion group.

1. The original title of *Mailbox* was *Racing for the Mailbox*. There are numerous references to the word mailbox throughout the novel. Are you surprised to know this particular chapter was pivotal in the novel's title? Why do you think Paul Mayer, the boy Sandy races to the mailbox, is such an important character?

2. Sandy is pre-occupied with the push-pull advance toward adulthood. In what scenes do you see her encouraging her reader-friend to cling to the innocence of childhood and in which scenes do you see her interest in embracing early adulthood. Do you think she feels that the pace of her own maturity is correct, or is she rushed toward adulthood in some way? Are children today held back or rushed forward more than previous generations?

3. Think about the passage where Sandy recommends writing letters to one's future self to fend off possible loneliness. How effective do you think her plan might be? Sandy has many friends, so why do you think she worries about future loneliness?

4. Sandy loves learning and sharing new words – their definitions and more subtle connotations. What do you learn of her and her development through words she specifically mentions? Examples might include: sin, tenacious, *tenir*, *chuchichaschtli*, *yakamoz*, onomatopoeia, bastard, dismay, bizarre, bazaar, priceless, *palabras*, *preguntas*, spontaneity, livid, unaccompanied minors, tremor, blemish, qwerty, waifishness, develop, sleuth, scapegoat, prone and supine. Which words are the most revealing of Sandy's character?

5. Are there certain foreign friends Sandy meets who have significant impact on her character? Do you think adults and children are equally capable of making foreign friends? Do you think adults or children are more capable and/or more interested in learning new languages?

6. Does Sandy trust male and female adults equally? Where do you find distinctions between the two?

7. Sandy is very observant of adults and adult behaviors. When Sandy observes the tan woman at the pool, what does she suppose a grown man might notice about this woman? What does she think most women would notice? Do you see other examples of Sandy's understanding of male versus female behaviors and position in society? How are Aunt Lula and Sandy's mother's perspectives similar or different?

8. Sandy mentions several books she especially likes. What do you make of her interest in the Nancy Drew Mysteries, *The Witch of Blackbird Pond*, the works of Judy Blume, and the E.L. Konigsberg novel *From the Mixed-up Files of Mrs. Basil E. Frankweiler*? Are

there more contemporary novels for young adults you would recommend to Sandy if she was a 13-year-old girl today? Do you think her negative opinion of Willa Cather's *My Antonia* is naïve?

9. In what sense do you think Sandy's understanding of the idea that she can be "nothing and everything and anything" begins to define her journey as a writer and as an adolescent?

10. Sandy Drue has been described as a "scrappy adolescent agnostic protagonist." Do you think she would agree with this description of herself, and if not, how do you think she might change the description? Would she change the description one way at the opening of the novel and another way at the end?

11. In Freund's debut novel *Rapeseed*, the protagonist is identified as a synesthete, a character with cross-wired or blended senses. She sees her letters and numbers in color, she senses various smells in association with certain colors and musical sounds. Do you see any evidence that Sandy Drue might also be a synesthcte? How important is the sense of smell in Sandy's experience? Taste? Texture? Temperature? Sound?

12. In "Facedown," Sandy's mother brings Barley with her when she hurries out to find Chris. Why do you think she brings Barley? Does Barley's absence in the house change the atmosphere when Sandy waits there alone? In what way does Barley play a role in the evening's events?

13. In what ways are Sandy's daily activities similar or different from those of an average 13-year-old today? How would you compare Sandy's parents' style of family management to parents of today? Is Sandy

burdened or benefitted by her parents' methodology? What about her brother Chris?

14. Do you feel that this novel was written for young adults, but adult readers are welcome to read it? Do you feel instead that it was written for adult readers, with young adults welcome to read it? Why?

About the Author

Nancy Freund was born in New York in 1966, raised in Kansas City, educated in Los Angeles, and married in London, England. Today she lives in Lausanne, Switzerland. She is the author of **Rapeseed** (2013, Gobreau Press) a *Foreword Reviews* finalist for Book of the Year in General Fiction. This critically acclaimed debut novel deals with expatriate life and synesthesia, the brain phenomenon of blended senses. In 2014, she published **Global Home Cooking: International Families' Favorite Recipes**. In 2013, her short story *Marcus* won the Geneva Writers first fiction prize, selected by American novelist Bret Lott. In 2014, she was a panelist and speaker at the Geneva Writers Group Conference and at the 13th International Conference for the Short Story in Vienna. Her writing has been published in *BloodLotus Journal*, *The Istanbul Review*, *Necessary Fiction*, *Offshoots*, *The Woolf*, and *The Daily Mail*. Freund has a BA in English and Creative Writing and a Masters from UCLA. She is active in community literacy for teens and adults. **Mailbox** is her second novel. Her third novel, **Effort of Will,** is forthcoming.

By all means, please connect:
www.nancyfreund.com
Twitter: @nancyfreund
Facebook: nancyfreundauthor
Pinterest: nancy freund
Goodreads: Nancy Freund